# INDEBTED DELIVERANCE

## MARCIA LYNN McCLURE

Published by Distractions Ink
1290 Mirador Loop N.E.
Rio Rancho, NM 87144

Published by Distractions Ink
©Copyright 2017 by M. Meyers
A.K.A. Marcia Lynn McClure
Cover Photography by © Ernie Ernst /Dreamstime.com
Cover Design and Interior Graphics
by Sandy Ann Allred/Timeless Allure

First Hardcover Edition: March 2017

McClure, Marcia Lynn, 1965—
*Indebted Deliverance:* a novella/by Marcia Lynn McClure.

ISBN: 978-0-9990831-2-3

Library of Congress Control Number: 2017944073

Printed in the United States of America

**To Kristy Jo...**
To old thrift store novels,
Rice Krispies treats for breakfast,
cashew clusters, and pralines.
But most of all...
To a friendship cherished in our memories
nestled warm in our hearts.
I miss you!

# CHAPTER ONE

"Why have you stopped?" Race Trevelian shouted. He grumbled with frustration, pounding on the inner roof of the carriage with one powerful fist.

"There seems to be some fracas barring the way, sir," the driver called.

"I am frozen to the bone, Rollins! Get this blasted thing moving!" Race demanded.

"The snow is far too deep on either side of the road to go around, sir," Rollins explained.

With an irate growl, Race opened the carriage door, stepping out into the frigid winter air. At once he saw that indeed Rollins was correct. There in the road, just in front of the horses and carriage, were three men struggling to restrain a young woman.

"Please help me, sir!" the girl begged.

"What the devil goes on here?" Race roared as his lengthy stride carried him toward the trespassers. Bearing down upon them, he recognized the men: the Cochran brothers. He felt his scowl deepen, for there were no more vile men in the country.

"None of your business, Trevelian!" one of the men answered, tightly clamping a hand over the girl's mouth.

"It is my business, Cochran," Race shouted, "for you're on my lands! Furthermore, you bar my way!"

"Leave it alone, Trevelian," another Cochran warned. "We'll be on our way soon enough."

"Do not make to threaten me. I'll rip your heart out with my bare hands," Race threatened. He thought for a moment that he would gladly sacrifice the well-being of his fine clothes if it meant he could pummel a Cochran or two.

Suddenly, the man holding the girl shouted, launched a string of profanity into the air as he removed his hand from her mouth. Race felt a grin tug at one corner of his mouth. It seemed the pretty chit had bitten her assailant.

"Please, sir," she begged—frantic. "I am abducted from my family this very day! Please do not allow them take me!"

Race glared at her, saying, "I care only to return to my home. This cursed snow has already closed the canyon for the winter...and you are no concern of mine." Turning to the man holding her, he commanded, "Move aside, Cochran, and let me pass. It matters not to me what you are about with the girl, but I intend to traverse this road, whether it is done by trampling over your dead corpse or not."

Race Trevelian knew the Cochrans would not trifle with his threats. Thus, as the girl continued to struggle, the filthy men dragged her to one side of the road, clearing the way for the carriage.

"As it should be," Race grumbled, returning to the carriage.

He climbed into the conveyance and knocked on the inner roof to signal Rollins to carry on. He did not bother glancing out the carriage window as it passed the girl, now left to the mercy of her abductors. He must return home immediately. The snow was beginning to fall once more; there was no time to dally.

"Halt, Rollins!" he shouted after a moment, however. Race growled as the carriage jolted to a jarring halt. Again he left the shelter of the carriage.

Grumbling to himself, he returned to the Cochrans and their hostage. "Release her, Cochran," he ordered.

The men looked to him, astonished—mouths agape.

"Who do you think you are, Trevelian?" one of them shouted.

"It is obvious that the chit does not wish to accompany you," Race said. "Therefore, release her, and allow her to return to her family."

The largest Cochran brother stepped forward. "Now, see here—" he began. Yet before he could utter another word, one mighty fist belonging to Race Trevelian met with his jaw—sending him sprawling to the ground.

Race advanced two steps forward and grabbed another Cochran head between his hands, forcing the face down to meet his knee. Tossing the man aside, he reached for the third—who instantly released the girl and turned to run. Yet Race grabbed the collar of his coat, yanking him back.

"I am not a man to be argued with," Race growled as he shoved the man facedown into the snow. "Make a move to stand, and I will show no mercy," he growled.

The third man obeyed. Race looked to the girl. She stood trembling, mouth gaping in awe. Reaching out, he none too gently took hold of her arm and began leading her toward the carriage.

"M-my home is the other direction, sir," the girl stammered.

"The snow will have blocked the canyon by now, and I have no intention of turning back. You will need to winter at my home and work to earn your keep until the snow melts in the spring," Race grumbled. He opened the carriage door, effortlessly lifting her and depositing her within. "Now sit still, and do not talk. I am in no humor for company."

"Thank you for—" the girl humbly began.

"I said keep silent, girl," Race reminded her.

The girl did as ordered then, snuggling into the comfort of the carriage seat in an attempt to warm her no doubt frigid body.

Chalyce LaSalle studied the angry, violent man sitting across from her and glaring out into the merciless weather. She had heard stories of the magnificent Race Trevelian—tales of his vast riches, violent temper, and, yes, unsurpassed good looks. Truly, he was as handsome as she had heard—even more so—and as ill-tempered. His eyes were as green as any emerald-eyed cat, and his hair was the blackest black she had ever seen. He was tall and broad-shouldered—mightily radiating the essence of strength.

Surely he was only in jest about Chalyce having to endure the winter at his home. She must return to her own family! How worried they would be, thinking the Cochrans had actually succeeded in taking her. She must return home! She must!

Carefully she ventured, "Sir…I simply must return home. My family will fear—"

"Perhaps your family would be far more alarmed to learn you are sheltering at my home than even that of the Cochrans," he said. "Come spring we will return you to your family. You may explain to them at that time and not before…for as I have already told you, girl, it is impossible to go back now."

"But I-I—"

"Furthermore, I will not listen to your insignificant babbling any longer," he interrupted, exhaling a heavy sigh of exasperation. "So please silence yourself…or *I* shall silence you."

"You have no right to speak so condescending, sir," Chalyce scolded. The great man before her was obviously surprised by her lack of obedience to his command—and was at a loss for words. "I am no less important or of any less value than you are."

"I delivered your life, girl!" he roared. "How dare you—"

"And I have already attempted to thank you for it, sir," Chalyce interrupted. "I am not averse to working through the winter in order to earn my keep, but I will not be treated with less respect than you would bestow upon a dog."

"Believe me...I would value a dog far more than I would an ungrateful child!" he growled. "And I am not averse to throwing you out of this carriage this moment and leaving you to the wolves! So fasten your patronizing little mouth, or I will make good my threat to do it for you."

"I am truly impressed, Mr. Trevelian," Chalyce said, the intonation of her voice thick with sarcasm. "You unquestionably are as vile as I have heard tell."

"Oh, I promise you, chit...you have no idea," he growled, finally intimidating her into silence.

Chalyce wiped the moisture from the carriage windowpane as it slowed to a stop. A massive log house loomed amid the forest trees. Warm light cascaded from its windows and out across the snow-covered ground. She watched as Race Trevelian shoved the carriage door open with his foot and stepped down, leaving her to exit on her own.

A man, appearing to be several years Trevelian's senior, approached. Chalyce listened as Race Trevelian issued instructions to the man.

"Fetch me a meal, Lyle. I'm ravenous," Race Trevelian grumbled. "Oh," he added, gesturing toward Chalyce, "and I've brought you something to keep you company these long winter months."

The man called Lyle arched one curious eyebrow as he nodded to Chalyce. Still staring at her, he addressed his employer, "We were wondering if you would make it back, sir."

"Find her something to do, Lyle. Anything. Just keep her out of my way," Race Trevelian grumbled.

The older man approached Chalyce then, offering his hand. "I'm Lyle, miss. We weren't expecting a…a guest."

"Neither was he," Chalyce assured him, accepting his hand. "I'm Chalyce LaSalle. Your employer rescued me from a truly wretched fate." Watching her angry rescuer stride intently into the house, she added, "I think."

"Well, then," Lyle began, gesturing toward the house, "it will be refreshing to have a beautiful young lady to gaze upon through all the winter. We are all men here, you realize."

"N-no…I did not." Chalyce was then even more uncertain of whether her situation had changed for the better.

"*Good* men, miss," Lyle assured her. "I see the uncertainty on your pretty face, and I assure you, only good men—even Mr. Trevelian. Unfriendly though he may be, he is a good and honorable gentleman."

"I will have to trust your word on that, Mr.…Mr.…"

"Lyle. Just Lyle," he said. "Now follow me into the house, if you please. You must be frozen through and through."

"Yes, thank you," Chalyce admitted as she followed him.

"I know Mr. Trevelian will speak nothing of this to me, miss," Lyle began as they entered the house. "Therefore, I must acquire my knowledge of what has transpired here from you, I'm afraid." Lyle turned, smiling to her. "How is it that you came to be riding in the carriage with him?"

Chalyce cast her gaze aside for a moment yet proudly raised her head as she answered, "You know of the Cochrans that live some ways from here?"

Lyle nodded—shook his head with obvious contempt. "Vile creatures...the entire family," he muttered.

"Yes," Chalyce agreed. "Well, you see...I've refused to be courted by the elder brother, Ernest. The entire family was vexed, and three of the brothers took it upon themselves to deliver me to their elder brother...against my will, of course. I was this very afternoon abducted from my own home...pulled mercilessly through the snow toward their dwelling. Mr. Trevelian came upon us struggling in the middle of the road and was vexed that we barred his way. I thought it certain he would leave me to them, but he must have a sliver of conscience in him somewhere, for he 'delivered' my life, as he himself put it. He assures me that the canyon is impassible by now and that I will have to winter here."

"That is most undeniably true, Miss LaSalle," Lyle confirmed. "We are snowbound here until at least April."

"April?" Chalyce exclaimed. "I cannot possibly remain here until April! That's more than five months!"

"More likely six."

"Six months?" she gasped.

"A disadvantage of living in the mountainous region…for some." Lyle lowered his voice, adding, "Perceived as a blessing to others."

Chalyce glanced up to see Race Trevelian fairly rip his coat from his body and fling into a nearby chair.

Immediately he began shouting orders to the two young men who greeted him when first he had entered the house ahead of Lyle and Chalyce. "Stable the horses! Inform Haynes that I have returned and wish to be nourished. Blasted cold! I assume the fire is roaring in the library?" His voice was deep and commanding—reverberated throughout the entryway.

Chalyce looked to Lyle, her brows arched in an expression of astonishment.

Lyle simply shrugged and said, "He's a brooding man."

"Brooding?" Chalyce whispered. "More precisely prideful and self-absorbed."

Lyle chuckled. "Ah, fair maiden. *Judge ye not that ye be not judged.* There's more to the pickle than the vinegar," he said, smiling. "Now, come along. You need warmth and nourishment. It is late now…but we will find a task for you to busy yourself with come morning."

Chalyce smiled at last. Lyle was intriguing. In the few minutes they had shared conversation, she had received a keen insight into his character—and she liked this person. He struck her as truly honest, utterly loyal, and somehow uncannily wise.

"Imagine," Lyle began as he poured hot cider into his employer's mug later that night, "finding such a pretty pastry…just there in the middle of the road."

Race Trevelian said nothing in response, simply stared into the fire burning in the hearth before him.

Hours earlier, Lyle had shown Chalyce to the room that would be hers. Now he and his employer were the only two people in the house that did not yet sleep. So it always was.

"She's got the look of an angel," Lyle commented.

"An imp, more likely," Race grumbled.

"Such brilliance in green eyes I've not seen since…well, since yours, sir."

"Wicked green. Spiteful and proud."

"And her hair…quite striking in its rare auburn tint."

"Yes…the hint of the she-devil, red."

Lyle smiled to himself—carefully studied his employer's countenance. "A complexion like porcelain."

"Not enough sun."

"Ah! But rosy cheeks and berry lips."

"Painted, no doubt."

Lyle's smile broadened. His employer rarely sparred at wits with him, and he found it intriguing.

"The frame is petite yet pleasantly curved," Lyle baited.

"Undeniably the runt of the litter," Race grumbled.

"Overall…an unusually beautiful young woman."

"A stubborn, ill-mannered, garrulous brat."

"And such a fascinating name…Chalyce. Unusual."

"A name more befitting a domesticated mongoose than a human being."

Lyle smiled. "I think I will retire, sir. Do you require anything else?"

"I require that you keep her out of my way, Lyle. I have no tolerance of people. Return her to her family when spring rears its ugly head. I wash my hands of her," Race responded.

The amused smile faded from Lyle's face as he exited the room. With one last look at his employer, he shook his head—disappointed.

આ

Lyle entered the library the following morning to find Race Trevelian asleep in the chair—just where he had left him when he had retired the night before. Race Trevelian rarely retired to his bed. He seemed to prefer the less comfortable seat before the fire.

"Good day, sir," Lyle spoke as Race's jade eyes opened, glaring at him.

"I doubt it, Lyle," Race mumbled as he rose to his feet.

"I am ready, Lyle. To earn my board here," Chalyce announced from the doorway.

Both men turned to see the fresh beauty standing just inside the room.

Chalyce looked from one man to the other, settling her gaze on Race Trevelian. "Those were your orders, were they not?" she asked.

"Indeed," he growled. "Occupy her, Lyle," he mumbled, rising from the chair. He rather pushed past Chalyce as he angrily strode from the room.

"He is an enormous man," Chalyce remarked.

"Yes…and powerful. The strength of ten men, I've no doubt," Lyle added.

"The brutality of ten is more closely the truth," Chalyce said.

Lyle raised his eyebrows—curious. Was the girl truly as indifferent to Race as she appeared? He wondered; thus he baited her. "Yet women find him brutally handsome all the same."

"I suppose," she began, "if one's preferences turn to scowling expressions and heartless words." Chalyce came to stand before Lyle, awaiting his instruction.

"Ah, but he caches a heart of gold beneath the ice."

"Of stone, no doubt," the girl countered once more. She smiled at him then, and Lyle was struck with the uncanny similarity between the conversation he had held with his employer concerning her the night before and the one he had only just experienced with her in regard to Race Trevelian. "What duties await me then this frigid winter morn?" she asked, smiling.

Lyle chuckled. "Well, at least you have accepted your predicament. I have a mind to make you housekeeper. I try my best…but dusting, polishing, and the like…well, my coordination does not seem adept to these tasks. I am too clumsy, I suppose…always breaking some thing or the other." Glancing around the room for a moment, he said, "You may begin in this very room. There are some beautiful furniture pieces, as you can see. It has been years since they have been cared for properly."

"That is an unusual rug, there before the fire," Chalyce commented.

"Peruvian...and very soft. I've seen nothing else like it," Lyle said. "You'll find dusting cloths and oils in the room off the kitchen. Stop in and have yourself some breakfast as you go through. Haynes is the cook...and a very good one at that. He is expecting you."

"Thank you, Lyle," Chalyce said. She smiled at him and started toward the kitchen.

Lyle chuckled as he watched her leave. Yes, this winter would prove very interesting—very interesting indeed.

Chalyce found Haynes to be a very congenial man. He was attractive, boasting pale hair and brown eyes— perhaps ten years her senior. He spoke comfortably with her as he served her a breakfast better sized for a man.

"Now, Race Trevelian...he does not often come home with a woman tucked under his wing," Haynes commented, smiling with suspicion as he poured milk into a glass for Chalyce.

"He did not tuck me under his wing, I assure you," Chalyce informed the man. "He simply rescued me from the elements…among other things…and rather grudgingly at that."

"And do you find him as irresistibly handsome as every other female on the face of this earth?" Haynes asked.

Chalyce choked slightly on the mouthful of milk she had begun to swallow.

Regaining her composure quickly, however, she answered, "He is sublimely handsome…and I would be a liar if I did not admit it. However, since you have chosen to be so forthright, so shall I. Mr. Trevelian a sadistic, selfish brute…whose very being seems void of compassion or concern for any other human save himself."

Haynes raised his eyebrows in obvious awe at such a judgment—and Chalyce felt almost scolded by his expression.

"Is he?" he asked. "And all this you have gathered from a mere few hours in his company?"

"He nearly left me to be…to be compromised by an entire band of degenerates!" she defended herself. "Then, after he had very reluctantly salvaged me—and I am certain he did so against his greater desires—he threatened to throw me to the wolves!"

Again Haynes's eyebrows raised in wonder. "Well, the mere fact that he took you into his protection at all...wouldn't that establish that he must possess some compassion?"

"Conscience does not require the company of compassion," Chalyce said. She quickly humbled herself, however—for in the end, he had saved her. "Still, I owe him my very life."

"And that is what vexes you," Haynes said.

"What do you mean by that?"

"You are indebted to him," he answered. "He delivered you from certain tragedy. People always despise those to whom they are indebted." She watched him as he wiped his flour-dusted hands on his trousers and considered the truth of his words.

"I do not despise him," Chalyce mumbled. "He is just...he is just so..."

"He will not expect you to repay the debt, Miss LaSalle, if that gives you further concern...even if it were possible to offer remuneration. Race Trevelian labors very hard to be the man that he appears to be."

"Do you and Lyle stay up nights concocting riddled defenses of your employer?" Chalyce asked.

Haynes chuckled. "No. But remember...we are they who know him best. We are not only his staff but his friends, and only company. We know him. We have seen him through…through many years. He is a good man…even if appearances lend to your belief otherwise."

"He pays you well, does he?" Chalyce asked, smiling.

Haynes chuckled, smiling as he studied Chalyce. She found she blushed under his gaze—for he was quite charming.

"You're a beautiful young woman, Miss LaSalle," he said. "I look forward to seeing you in my kitchen each morning this winter."

As he winked at her before returning to the stove, Chalyce bit her lip—delighted by his kindness and charisma. She liked this man, as well as Lyle. Whatever could be their reasons for such compassionate loyalty to a brute the likes of Race Trevelian.

# CHAPTER TWO

Days passed, and Chalyce had not again even glimpsed the master of the house in which she now dwelt. She was an independent, determined young woman and had reconciled herself to enduring the winter in the home of Race Trevelian. Still, her curiosity was aflame where the handsome, brooding, seemingly heartless man was concerned. Furthermore, she sensed that some dark or mysterious secret lay hidden within the strong, snowbound house—and that all who dwelt within were coupled with it—save herself.

Lyle was an attractive man with distinguished, graying temples and a warming smile—a person of interest—and Chalyce was always pleased with his company. He seemed quite knowledgeable about nearly every subject she could think to bring to his attention. Thus, she fancied that he was a well-educated man.

Haynes was flirtatious, handsome, and friendly. He complimented her endlessly, and she was quite flattered by his attentions.

Chalyce had also become acquainted with the other two men who labored in Race Trevelian's employ. Marcus Young tended the horses and other stock on the property. He was a quiet, shy sort and rarely spoke. Peter Rollins was the man who had driven the carriage that brought Chalyce to the house. He tended to many other matters as well, including upkeep of the house and grounds.

The fourth morning after her arrival, Chalyce was dusting in one of the bottom floor rooms when she heard a loud crashing sound from the direction of the entryway. Rushing into the entry, she stopped, gasping as she beheld a tremendous tree limb lying on the floor inside the house. Beneath it lay the slivered glass of the window through which it had fallen. Bitterly cold wind and snow were blowing into the house. Lyle and Haynes were there—staring with disbelief at the wreckage.

"What a racket!" Race Trevelian growled, appearing from the library. His boots crushed the slivered glass as he strode toward the limb. "Well, don't just stand there looking at it! We must cover the window and haul away the debris!" he bellowed.

Chalyce watched as Race Trevelian reached down, hefting the enormous limb onto his broad shoulders. Striding to the broken window, he tossed the wayward timber out into the riotous elements from whence it came.

Turning back to meet the startled faces staring at him, he shouted, "Have I left my trousers behind? No? Then assist me!"

At once Lyle left the room, voicing his intentions of retrieving a broom.

"Bring Peter in here as well, Lyle. We will have to secure this blasted window somehow," Race called after him. Chalyce felt her entire body grow warm as his attention fell to her. "You have nothing to attend to?" he asked, frowning at her.

"I-I was dusting," she stammered. Oh, how he suddenly unsettled her! She usually prided herself on her calm head and wit, but this man muddled her brain. In just the four days since she had last seen him, she had somehow quite forgotten how unsettlingly attractive he was.

"Dusting?" he asked, still scowling at her. "Is it not apparent that dusting can be put off for a moment? Now bring me that bucket, brat," he ordered, pointing to a bucket sitting on the floor near to where she stood. The bucket had been placed so as to catch the occasional drops of water dripping from a point in the ceiling.

Chalyce picked up the bucket and went to stand next to him.

"This glass," he mumbled as he hunkered down and began picking up pieces of the shattered windowpane and dropping them into the bucket.

Chalyce bent down, reaching for a piece in an attempt to help him. Yet he caught her hand in his own. She glanced up to see him glaring at her.

"You do not want to take to bleeding all over the only dress you have, do you?" he asked.

Snatching her hand from his grip, she looked to him with defiance. "I am not a clumsy fool. And besides...what difference would it make to you if I ruin my dress?" Chalyce reached for a piece of the glass, taking it carefully in hand and depositing it into the bucket.

"I doubt any of us here have a pair of trousers that would fit you," he growled. "Your only alternative would then be to spend the winter *dusting* in your petticoats." He winced as a piece of the shattered glass cut his palm. His eyes narrowed, and he ordered, "Not one word."

Chalyce arched one brow—bit her lower lip in an attempt to conceal the amused grin threatening to display itself.

Wiping his hand on his shirt and smearing it with blood, he continued to pick up bits of glass and deposit them into the bucket. Periodically, he would press the wound to his chest, leaving another stain on the once immaculate shirt.

"I assume you have more than one shirt to winter in…considering you have fully ruined the one you are wearing," Chalyce could not keep herself from commenting.

"Impertinent brat," he growled.

At that moment, Peter Rollins burst through the front door. "Mr. Trevelian! I think that old tree is going to fall in the direction of the house!" he exclaimed.

Race stood and without a word strode out through the front door, ripping the large ax from Peter's hands as he exited.

"What does he intend to do?" Chalyce asked, going to stand next to Peter. She watched as Race entered the wind and blowing snow unprotected and began chopping at the trunk of an enormous tree grown near the front of the house.

"That tree," Peter began, pointing to the tree Race was attacking with the ax, "is older than the hills. The branch that broke this window broke from it. It's creaking something terrible in this storm, and I fear it will land on the house if we do not fell it."

Chalyce watched as Race's breath manifest itself as a small space of fog in the frigid air. Each stroke of the ax lethally met the tree, accompanied by a low grunt from the man wielding it. And then—after several long minutes—Chalyce heard a loud, ominous crackling sound as the tree began to fall. It hit the ground with enormous force—and in opposition of the house.

Race returned to the house, slamming the door behind him. His breathing was labored, and his face and hands were reddened from the cold. He returned the ax to Peter, who took it—careful to avoid the blood on the handle left by the wound in Race's hand.

"We'll split it into firewood as soon as the storm blows over," Race said. "Now, let us dispose of this debris."

Lyle returned, and Chalyce thought it had taken him an exorbitant amount of time to retrieve a broom. "What was that blasted noise outside? It sounded as if the entire house was falling in," he said.

"We felled that tree out front, Lyle. That's all," Race explained. "We should have done it long ago."

Chalyce assisted the others in sweeping up the glass and mopping the moisture caused by the melting snow that blew in as the men worked to board up the window. Race, however, had disappeared up the stairs after felling the tree. It would be days more before Chalyce would see him again.

"He's very reclusive," Chalyce said, enjoying a hearty breakfast Haynes had prepared for her. It has been nearly two weeks since the tree limb had broken the window—yet Chalyce had seen Race Trevelian only on the rare occasion.

"Yes," Haynes said. "More so since you've arrived."

"I feel so guilty over the imposition…my intrusion on his solitude," she explained. "Yet I cannot bear to think what my lot would've been at the hands of the Cochrans had they succeeded."

"No doubt. They're a family of thieving miscreants."

Chalyce smiled as she bit into one of Haynes's delicious spiced cakes. "Mmm," she sighed. "You do surprise me at times, Haynes. These are far too tasty for my figure."

Haynes sat down in a chair across the table from Chalyce, dropped his voice to a whisper, and said, "I doubt any amount of indulgence could spoil that figure, Chalyce."

She blushed and smiled at his flirt. "It is all too obvious you are a flatterer. My mother warns me about men like you, you know."

"And a wise woman she is too," he chuckled. "Now, I have a task for you. Run out to the smokehouse and bring in a ham, would you? I have things to tend to in here."

"Certainly," Chalyce chimed. She stood from her chair and retrieved her coat from a hook near the kitchen door. "I'll be back in a moment," she said.

She buttoned her coat and exited the house by way of the kitchen door.

The smokehouse was not far from the main house, and the stillness of the morning air was refreshing—even for its cool temperature. As Chalyce neared the smokehouse, she caught sight of Marcus, splitting wood.

"Good morning," Chalyce called to Marcus. He did not hear her, however, for he was some distance from her. She watched a moment as he continued to split wood—astounded he would be doing so wearing only his trousers and boots. She was fascinated by the movements of the enormous muscles of his arms and back as he worked. Still, Chalyce had seen her own father split wood in winter without a coat. It was a laborious task after all and no doubt found a body well heated. She frowned a moment, having never before noticed how very large Marcus was. Then again, she had not often spoken much to him.

Realizing she had not excreted much effort in offering greetings to him, she started toward him calling, "Good morning, Marcus. I see you are already hard at work this morning. And how do you find this crisp winter's…" Her words expired in her throat as the man ceased his chopping and turned to face her.

"F-forgive me, Mr. Trevelian. I did not realize..." she stammered.

"You have interrupted me now...so you may as well finish your question," he breathed, wiping perspiration from his brow.

Chalyce could see his breath manifest in the cold winter air and again marveled that he was outside working in only his trousers and boots.

"You're bound to catch your death, Mr. Trevelian," she said. "You're not properly dressed for—"

"Where are you bound, Chalyce?" he asked with obvious impatience.

"The smokehouse. Haynes has sent me out for—"

"Then pivot your little body just now and walk forward," he grumbled. "You'll walk straight into it that way."

"Thank you, sir," she said—though she well knew her way to the smokehouse. "You really should dress properly for the cold, you know," she added simply to goad him.

"You are something near a hireling here, Chalyce. Do not make to reprimand me."

"It was not my choice to be…your hireling, Mr. Trevelian. Granted you pulled me from the clutches of ruination. However, it was the lustful ambitions of the male species that placed me in such a predicament in the first of it. Your thwarting the intentions of those disgusting Cochrans and allowing me shelter for the winter in your home does not give you the right to treat me with such ill-mannered rudeness. After all, you are of the same gender as those who first abducted me, and—"

"I may be of the same gender, as you put it…but not of the same mind or intentions," he growled. "Especially where you are concerned."

Chalyce clenched her teeth. He was provoking her to being ill-tempered and defensive. "I have no doubt of that," she said. "It's obvious you have absolutely no interest in women, as I see it. Have you? Why else would you barricade yourself in this isolated house, surrounded by only male employees and—"

Before Chalyce could even think to move, he was upon her. Grabbing her by the wrist, he pulled her to face him—his angry emerald gaze burning into her own.

"What do you imply?" he asked through clenched teeth.

Chalyce could feel the inclination toward being intimidated rising within her—threatening to vanquish her courage.

Still, bravely she met his stare and said, "I only think it odd that you have no female employees here. A male cook, male housekeeper—"

"You arrogant little chit!" he rumbled. "You assume because I do not surround myself with spiteful, vindictive women…do not choose to seduce your vain little person…that I am emasculated somehow?" He pushed her backward in slight, pressing her back against one outer wall of the house and holding her there.

"That is not what I said. I only—" she began.

"Your implication was clear," he growled. "Believe me when I tell you, girl, that just because Ernest Cochran, the lowest form of human being, found you worthy of abduction…do not assume that every man would see you as irresistibly tempting…especially me."

"Let go of me, you ice-blooded reptilian brute!" Chalyce cried. In that moment, her courage abandoned her—for she knew his power and physical strength could render her helpless.

"Oh, I am as hot-blooded as the next man, brat," he mumbled. "Make no mistake about that. I simply choose from among a higher caliber of *your* gender. Furthermore, I prefer women…as opposed to naive little girls."

"Fat, wrinkled-up, old crones, no doubt? The only women who would have the likes of you, no doubt," she countered, meeting his angry stare with defiance.

His eyes narrowed as he studied her a moment. "Hmm," he breathed. "I wonder…do you want to feel a man's blood boiling? Is that it, little one?" he asked, dropping his voice to a whisper. He took her hands and forced their palms to the bareness of his massive chest. He bent, letting his mouth hover a breath from hers. "Do you want me to warm your young girl's blood? Ravish you with the heated kisses of my warm, moist mouth? Is that what you want?"

Chalyce was astonished at the sudden mad pounding of her heart—mortified at her body's trembling at being so near to his. Ripping one hand from his grasp, she slapped him soundly across one cheek.

"How dare you speak of such things to me!" she cried—though, in truth, his words had sent a strange and unfamiliar thrill racing through her.

Race Trevelian only chuckled—and Chalyce was instantly enchanted by the sheer magnificence of his smile. So astonished was she by the change his smile brought to his countenance that she was unable to react when his mouth suddenly met hers with such a driven force as to send a pure and breathtaking delight throughout her entire being! Her thoughts were momentarily scattered—yet she quickly regained her composure and commenced with struggling.

He indeed broke the potent seal of their lips, whispering, "I am the absolute essence of all that a man should be." His mouth lingered only a breath from hers as he added, "The supreme illustration of masculinity."

"Y-you flatter yourself," Chalyce stammered in a whisper.

He chuckled once more, however. "No. I think not. And your youth's blood, now heated by the boil of mine…affirms it."

"I loathe the very sight of you," Chalyce said.

Race arched an eyebrow. "Really?" he asked with obvious cynicism. "I do not think so, brat. The only thing keeping you from me is your woman's pride. Else you would have been thus occupied from the first moment you arrived."

Again Chalyce slapped him. He countered by taking her hands and pinning them at her back with one of his own. He held her body against the wall with his own—holding her chin steady with his theretofore unoccupied hand as his mouth claimed hers once more. His kiss was driven—demanding, heated, and moist—and Chalyce struggled. Yet he was too powerful, his body too strong for hers to have hope of escape. Again he kissed her and again until—whether for the fact she knew she must succumb in order to have hope of escape or whether the undeniable wonder of his kiss won over her good sense—Chalyce found she was suddenly in acceptance of his mouth to hers. She was breathless—weakened—yet simultaneously aloft on wings of bliss! For all her claiming to find Race Trevelian cruel and unattractive, she inwardly admitted to herself it was merely her manner of protecting herself from his profound and inexplicable allure! And then, for all the dominating essence of his kiss, Chalyce fancied they were tinged with something else—a scarcely restrained passion, hinting at tenderness. As his adept mouth threatened to overpower her will, thereby inducing her to surrender to him, a terrible pain unexpectedly punctured her heart. Tears escaped her eyes to travel down her face: tears of strange compassion, tears of longing. She had been given a glimpse into the depths of his soul. In those moments, she truly felt a torment and pain buried somewhere deep within him. It had touched her—for she somehow knew his hidden pain was most torturous.

Race ended the kiss—gazed down at her. His amused smile had vanished, yet he whispered, "There is nothing to be ashamed of, Chalyce," he mumbled. "It is instinctive, after all."

"Stop!" Chalyce cried in a whisper. Yet she found she had no strength with which to offer argument.

"I will barter with you," he said. "Spend these remaining winter nights in my…um…my company. Agree, and you may give up your household duties for more favorable ones." He chuckled, releasing her as she gasped in horror at his inference. "Now, run along to the smokehouse, brat. However, if you should reconsider…the offer stands."

His laughter echoed through the cold air as she trudged through the snow toward the smokehouse.

"He's bluffing, I tell you," Lyle chuckled later that evening. "Call his hand, Chalyce. I swear to you on my life there is no more honorable or moral a man on this earth than Race Trevelian."

"I am not inventing this, Lyle," Chalyce assured him. "He truly said those things to me!"

Lyle's face went solemn then. His voice dropped to barely a whisper. "He is trying to keep you frightened of him, Chalyce. You'll stay away from him that way, and he well knows it."

"I stay away from him all the same, Lyle," Chalyce reminded.

"Apparently not far enough."

Chalyce shook her head in frustration. "You all own some unfathomable loyalty toward him. You would never darken his good name."

"And rightly so, for he has done nothing to deserve it," Lyle stated with emphatic assurance.

"He forced himself upon me this very day, Lyle!" she reminded him.

"Forgive me, Chalyce…but he did no more than kiss you. And, forgive me again, but did you truly wish for escape from it?" Chalyce sighed with frustration. "Call his bluff, Chalyce. If you do not believe me…then call his bluff."

"You mean…offer myself to him?" she whispered in disbelief of Lyle's suggestion.

Lyle nodded. "Yes. I promise you…he will irrefutably refuse."

"I want you to know, Lyle," she began, "that I do not see myself as some great beauty, capable of winning any man. I only know that he is reclusive. Any old crone would no doubt be attractive to him."

"You are mistaken on both counts, Chalyce," Lyle said, smiling.

❧

It was very late. Lyle, Haynes, Peter, and Marcus had all retired for the night—Chalyce had made certain of it before venturing into the library. As was his nightly ritual, Race sat in the large chair before the hearth and fire.

"I have decided to accept your offer," Chalyce announced from behind him.

"What?" Race asked, standing to face her. "What are you about at this hour?"

At the sight of his shirt gaping open, displaying his broad, masterfully sculpted chest, Chalyce felt her knees begin to weaken as her courage threatened to flee.

"Y-your offer of earlier today," she stammered. "Your offer that I might exchange my house duties for…for others."

Race drew a deep breath, and Chalyce saw his jaw tightly clench. "Very well. We begin here…now," he said, motioning for her to stand before him.

Chalyce nearly turned to flee, but instinct told her Lyle had been right. She had called his bluff, and he was, in turn, calling hers. She walked to him until she stood directly in front of him. She looked up, and he stood stalwart—gazing down with indifference.

"I am yours. Do with me what you will," she whispered—hoping her confidence in Lyle's assurances had not been ill-placed.

"Very well," he muttered, and she watched—feigning apathy—as he stripped the shirt from his body, letting it drop to the floor. He motioned with one hand for her to move closer, and she did so. Taking her waist between his powerful hands, he slowly drew her against him.

The euphoric thrill that erupted within her at the first meeting of his mouth with hers caused Chalyce to quiver. As his kiss grew in deepening strength, her determination surrendered, and she rewarded him with willing, passionate responses. This time, the hint of tenderness was all the more evident. His mouth played with hers gently at first—then growing demanding—voracious. However, he seemed to be considerate of her tender body, even as his grip tightened around her waist—his thumbs pressing to her ribs—willing her to allowing her own hands to caress him.

"You want me to show you my hand, is that it?" he whispered as he tore his mouth from hers, abruptly releasing her. Chalyce's mind was still whirling, and she looked away to hide her blush. "Very well. You win. Your virtue is safe with me," he said. "Yet you knew that already, did you not?"

"Why do you appear so cruel?" she asked—still breathless.

"For the sake that I am cruel," he answered. "Now toddle off to your cradle, brat. You have nothing that I want. Believe me...I would take it if you did," he muttered, pushing past her.

Chalyce watched him stride away. "What wounded you so?" she asked in a whisper.

# CHAPTER THREE

Chalyce was still fatigued when she awoke the next morning. She had not rested well, for her mind had been muddled with thoughts of possibilities pertaining to the attitude—the very manner—of Race Trevelian.

She had sensed something again the night before when he had kissed her and was certain a deep wound bled within him. Thus, her mind was distracted, preoccupied with wondering what could possibly explain it all—the wound—his selfish, hateful facade.

Thus, as she sat across the table from Lyle at breakfast, she asked, "What happened to him, Lyle?"

"To what do you refer, Chalyce?" Lyle inquired. He did not look at her—simply continued to eat his morning meal.

"I believe you know perfectly well what I mean. What happened to Race Trevelian to turn him into such an uncaring, hateful man? Tell me."

"Nothing happened to him," Lyle said, still not meeting her gaze. "He is simply a private sort of man."

Chalyce sighed with exasperation. "You're protecting some deep, dark secret...are you not?"

"No...and I do not know what has planted the notion in your head that—"

"Oh, come now, Lyle!" Race exclaimed from the doorway then. "Tell her. Tell her all of it!"

Chalyce turned—watched him as he strode into the room. "I didn't mean to pry, Mr. Trevelian," she began. "I only—"

"Oh! Pry away, brat," he growled, his eyes narrowing as he glared at her. He sat down at the table with them. "In truth, Chalyce...it is all rather gothic and mysterious," he began. Leaning over so that his face was only inches from her own, he whispered, "You see...I have a lunatic wife hidden in the attic." Chalyce's eyes widened, and he continued, "No...no...it is my leprous mother hidden in the basement. Isn't that it, Lyle?" Lyle grinned as Chalyce inhaled an impatient breath—irritated with herself at being so gullible. "Wait," Race persisted. "Rather it is the harem of mistresses I keep in the secret rooms. Yes! That's it! Yes…I have a plethora of loose women hidden away that tend to my every…whim."

"I like the leprous mother story best," Chalyce said.

"Very well then. I have a leprous mother rotting away in the basement," Race said. "I have only just come from bidding her a good morning. You may cease in interrogating poor Lyle…for I am afraid that the only skeletons hidden here are those that your very gullible mind can create."

Haynes placed a plate of food on the table before Race.

"Haynes," Race began, "did you know that Lyle and our young brat have been scheming behind my back?"

"Really, sir?" Haynes inquired with indifference.

"Oh, yes. You see, Chalyce—well, how can I put this delicately? Chalyce wishes to be my—oh, how can I say it?—my kept woman, as it were."

Chalyce gasped, "What?"

"It's true, Haynes," Race continued, however. "And Lyle, I fear, has encouraged this. Isn't that so, Lyle?"

Lyle raised guilty brows. Yet Chalyce flew to her own defense. "How dare you? That is a lie! An utter and very heinous lie!"

"I have refused, of course," Race said, paying her no heed. "In fact, it came to my mind only this morning that perhaps the fracas with the Cochrans in the road was only a ploy to deliver the brat into my home, thereby allowing her the opportunity to…entice me…trap me into marriage. Was that the plan?" Race's glare burned into Chalyce's.

"He is a gargoyle, Lyle!" Chalyce exclaimed. "How can you defend him as being a good man?" She looked to Haynes then, her expression pleading for assistance. "Haynes…do you hear his accusations toward me?" When Haynes did not respond, however, Chalyce looked to Lyle and back. "What does he hold over the both of you? Surely it is not simply misplaced loyalty that holds you to him!" Chalyce rose to her feet, still glancing from one man to the other in expectation of an explanation.

"Sit down, Chalyce. You're upsetting my stomach," Race calmly ordered.

Chalyce was enraged. She was absolutely aware of the jesting expressions now apparent on each of the three faces before her. Still, to make light of such matters was unendurable. Picking up the plate of food Haynes had placed before Race, she smashed it against his chest—smearing his immaculate white shirt with strawberry preserves, eggs yolks, and bacon grease.

"Oh my," Lyle muttered as he watched Race slowly rise from his chair.

"How dare you slander me so?" Chalyce scolded. "Accusing me of…of…"

"You little imp!" Race growled. Violently he tore open his soiled shirt, sending buttons flying throughout the room. Wadding it up, he threw it at her feet.

Chalyce gulped as she looked up into his enraged expression. His massive chest rose and fell with his angered breathing. Ceremoniously, he wiped his chest with one hand—studied the contents of his breakfast that had soaked through his shirt to his skin.

"I-I am sorry," Chalyce apologized. "You provoked me."

Race nodded in acknowledgment. "Perhaps," he mumbled. Then, taking hold of her arm, he said, "Even so…you will clean up this mess you have made."

"Unhand me," Chalyce demanded, attempting to free her arm from his grasp. "I will wash your confounded shirt if that is what you want."

"The shirt is ruined...beyond repair. I meant *this* mess," he explained, pointing to his muscular torso.

Chalyce's eyes widened, her mouth falling agape as she realized the meaning of his insinuation. "You cannot be in earnest!"

"You clean it...else I will rub your nose in it like a puppy needing house training!" he growled.

Chalyce looked to Lyle for support, but he only smiled, shrugging his shoulders. Haynes looked far less amused but made no move to champion her.

"I am sorry, Mr. Trevelian," Chalyce repeated. "It was a childish act, I admit, but—"

"Let me direct you to the washbasin," he said, pulling her in the direction of it. He handed her a cloth. "Clean it up," he ordered.

Chalyce's first inclination was to pick up the basin full of water and promptly empty it over his head. However, she doubted she could skillfully raise the heavy basin to such a height that the deed would require, so she soaked the cloth in the water at hand and wrung it out. She glanced up to him and thought she caught a glimpse of a grin on his face—but it vanished before she could be certain she had even seen it there. Still, too unsure as to whether he was truly vexed or simply teasing, she wrung the cloth tighter.

As Race held his arms outstretched at his side, Chalyce took a deep breath and began wiping the breakfast residues from his impressive form. Thoughts of the evening before began to fill her mind—the warmth of his body as he had held her against it—the warm taste of his passionate kisses.

"It was a wise choice," he began, "choosing not to douse me with the water."

Chalyce tossed the cloth into the basin. "You're immaculate once again," she told him. "May I go? I have far less revolting things to attend."

"I am still damp. Do you plot to inflict me with pneumonia?" he asked.

"No, of course not," Chalyce said.

"Then dry," he commanded, offering a dry cloth to her.

Gritting her teeth to subdue the furious words threatening to escape her lips, she snatched the towel from him.

"Why, you are correct, Mr. Trevelian," she said. "We certainly cannot have you running about wet in midwinter, can we?" As an impish grin curled her lips, she placed the cloth to his chest and began rubbing as roughly and as briskly as she could, intending to inflict him with discomfort. She was stopped as his hand gripped her wrist.

"Thank you," he said. "You may go. But bind that impulsive temper of yours...lest you wish to continue cleaning up after yourself."

Chalyce tossed the cloth to the floor next to his soiled shirt. "I am not at all sure which would be the least desirable to endure—leaving here to endure braving the elements in an attempt to reach my home...or sheltering under a roof with the likes of you. Either choice is frigid and unendurable." She looked up again, this time certain she had seen him force a playful smile from his face.

Race glared at her. "You know the way to the front door."

"Yes. But I fear that I am more of a coward than I would like to admit."

"Enough. I have no time for this horseplay," he growled, his patience obviously spent. "Lyle, I will be out this evening, as you well know. See that all is in readiness," Race ordered before striding out of the room.

"You! Both of you!" Chalyce scolded as she glared at the innocent expressions of Lyle and Haynes. "He is a brute! And neither one of you made one move to help me. How could you allow him abuse me so?"

The two men looked at one another, smiling.

It was Lyle who spoke first. "He was only taunting, Chalyce. Horseplay was all it was," he explained.

Chalyce's eyes widened. "He forced me to bathe his...his...and you're trying to tell me that this is his way of amusing himself?" She shook her head, entirely perplexed by the goings-on. Remembering the last words Race had spoken, however, she cooled her temper and inquired, "And anyway...where could he possibly be going tonight? We are snowbound on the mountain!"

Though neither Lyle nor Haynes offered explanation, Chalyce did not miss the look of conspiracy that passed between them.

"He...he is attending a friend," Lyle answered.

"You are lying," she accused. "I do not believe the man has a friend in the world. How could he?"

"It is true, Chalyce," Haynes confirmed. "He is indeed going visiting."

A disturbing thought entered into her mind—and she voiced it. "A woman friend?"

"Helena Dickson lives on a neighboring property," Lyle muttered. "Each month, Race makes the trek to her home to make certain all is well."

Chalyce noted the tone of resentment apparent in Lyle's voice.

"How interesting," she mused aloud. "One would think, being the recluse that he is, that the anticipation of spending an evening with a woman would find him in a somewhat more amiable frame of mind. Yet he seems contrary…more ill-tempered than even is typical."

"I've got chores to tend to," Haynes said, his desire to elude further discussion on the subject far too evident.

"As do I," Lyle added as he nearly raced from the room.

❧

"I will be late, Lyle…as always," Race grumbled as he fastened the buttons on his heavy coat.

Chalyce noted how gloomy he appeared. "Enjoy yourself," she could not help calling as he began to leave.

Turning, he glared—his jade eyes spewing venom in her direction. "If I am fortunate, I will come upon a criminal hid out in the woods. He will murder me, and I will neither arrive at my destination nor return home afterwards." Chalyce's mouth fell agape at the vehemence of his words. "Yet fear not, brat. Luck has never been my companion."

Very late that night, Chalyce lay awake in her bed— listening for any sound that may indicate Race's return. She had been lying awake for hours, her mind concocting plots and vivid images of Race's visit to the woman known as Helena. She wondered if the woman were a great beauty. Perhaps she too had some odd, misplaced loyalty to the Race Trevelian. Chalyce thought it more likely, however, that Race had some deep sense of duty toward her. Could it be some lewd secret such as an illegitimate child conceived during one of his visits? Blackmail perhaps? As her mind was thus occupied, she heard his footsteps on the stairs. Quietly, she crept to her door, placing one ear firmly against it—and then there were voices.

"All is unchanged?" she heard Lyle ask.

"Precisely," Race growled.

"I am sincerely sorry, Race," Lyle added.

"Do not be. We reap what we sow, after all."

At that moment, the door to Chalyce's room—which had not been tightly shut—closed, producing an audible noise. Gasping, she backed away from the door as she heard heavy footsteps approach. In an instant, the door was flung open, revealing a furious Race Trevelian.

"Am I to lose every degree of my privacy to your curiosity, brat?" he roared.

"Off with you now, sir. The hour is late," Lyle coaxed. "We disturbed her...that is all."

"I-I heard voices. They woke me," Chalyce stammered.

Yet Race lunged forward, taking her chin in hand. "Did they?" he asked. Without warning, he pulled her face to his—kissing her with such driven claim that she feared she may smother in it. Yet she did not struggle or make to evade him, for she sensed the aching need in him. Not a need of any physical, lustful nature—rather that of a tortured soul in search of deliverance.

"Sir...Race. Stop. You are not yourself," Lyle calmly scolded.

Abruptly releasing her face, Race muttered, "No. I am not. Nor have I been for some time, Lyle...as well you know."

Chalyce was startled to see Haynes suddenly appear behind Race. He took hold of his employer's arm, turning him away from her.

"Being master of this house does not give you the right to force your attentions on our guest!" Haynes growled.

Chalyce was unsettled by the expression of malice apparent on Haynes's face. She watched Race's jaw repeatedly clench and release with restrained aggression.

"And employment in the house over which *I* am master...does not give you allowance to reprimand me," Race growled. "Mind your place, Haynes...else you will have none here," he threatened.

"You have been attending to Helena this evening, Trevelian. Do not make to continue your dalliance now with Chalyce," Haynes said.

Race drew a deep breath. Chalyce watched as every visible muscle in his body tensed.

"If it were anyone but you, Haynes...you would be dead where you stand," he said. Without uttering one word more, he left the room.

Chalyce stood watching him go, but her attention was suddenly arrested by the conversation now taking place between Lyle and Haynes.

"I cannot believe you would say the likes to him, Haynes," Lyle reprimanded in a lowered voice.

"Hhhmm," Haynes scoffed. "He cannot be allowed to torment every woman on earth simply because…" He paused—glanced at Chalyce. He then pointed to her as he continued speaking to Lyle. "There is a fine line indeed between seduction and assault, my friend."

"He is an impulsive man who in constant labors to restrain a great anger and heavy guilt, Haynes. Furthermore, your implications where Helena Dickson is concerned…" Lyle shook his head. "It was an absolute act of cruelty on your part."

Haynes looked to Chalyce, frowning. "You are the victim here, Chalyce. What say you?" he asked her. "He bursts in upon you in the middle of the night, using you for his own pleasure at a whim! Tell Lyle that I was right in my accusation!"

Chalyce sighed—softly answered, "He did nothing that I did not allow, Haynes."

"What?" Haynes roared.

"If the two of you would see your way clear to tell me what is really going at play here…I may be at less of a disadvantage in these situations," she spat with vexation.

"What situations?" Haynes asked. "Do you mean to say he has done this before?"

"I mean in situations where he seems to nearly lose his senses with frustration and pent-up anger, Haynes. That is all," she answered.

The expression of secrecy that had become so familiar to her passed between the two men again.

"Very well," she concluded, realizing she would receive no further information. "I wish to attempt to get some rest this night. If you do not mind, gentlemen," she said, pointing to the door.

Haynes left in a rather perturbed manner. Lyle, however, paused before leaving.

He looked to Chalyce—an almost pained expression of pleading in his face. "He's a good man, Chalyce," he said. "It is not my place to tell you more than that. Do you understand?"

Chalyce smiled and sighed—for she did feel compassion toward Lyle. His hiding whatever knowledge he owned of his employer's past was almost certainly as destructive to Lyle as the secret he kept was to Race.

"I know, Lyle," she whispered.

Lyle smiled, reassured. He left then, closing the door behind him.

# CHAPTER FOUR

The weeks passed at winter's own gloomy, monotonous pace. Race continued to visit Helena Dickson each month, always returning late into the night—broody and angry—easily provoked the following few days.

However, Chalyce had ceased to judge his manner—had begun to observe him from a different perspective. She had discovered that, although his wit was often undetectable at first, it was wildly original. He indulged a great deal in what Lyle referred to as "horseplay"—often only verbal, yet just as often physical. Also, though his attempts at physical contact with her had ceased following the night he had burst into her bedchamber, his spoken flirtations had increased. Chalyce noticed this caused a great uneasiness to develop between Haynes and Race—

mostly emanating from Haynes—and she suspected this was Race's reason for offering such remarks.

It was, in fact, late November when the tension between the two men reached its pinnacle. Chalyce had ventured once more out into the elements to fetch something from the smokehouse. As she passed the chopping block, she could not keep her gaze from wandering to the place—remembering the instance when Race had cornered her—kissed her for the first time. As she thought back on the occasion, her body began to tingle—thrilled at the memory of the sensation his kiss had caused to course through her.

Hurriedly, she entered the smokehouse and began to search for the item Haynes had requested. She was startled, however, when the door to the smokehouse suddenly slammed closed behind her. Turning, she saw Haynes stood in the small shelter with her.

"Haynes!" she exclaimed, giggling with relief. "You scared the breath out of me!" Chalyce shook her head—returned to her task. "I do not find any smoked salmon out here. Are you certain you yet have reserves?"

"Oh, I am quite sure I do not, Chalyce," he chuckled.

At the sinister intonation of his voice, Chalyce felt every hair on her head prickle with anxiety.

"Well, then…I suppose we can go on back to the house," she said. Her heart's beat was quickening—with fear. As she tried to move past him, he took hold of her arm, stalling her.

"Not yet, lovey," he mumbled.

"Haynes…let me pass," she said—feigning courage.

He did not release her, however. "Now, the way I see things…I've kept my distance for long enough, Chalyce," he said. "You and I…we've become good friends, have we not?"

"Yes, Haynes…we are good friends," she answered. "Thus, let us ensure the continuance of that association."

"Yet I have been thinking…" he continued, taking hold of her other arm. His grip was viselike, and her anxiety grew. "Perhaps I misjudged Race that night in your room weeks ago. Now that I think back on it…you did not make one move to stop his advances toward you. Thus, I think it is time I tried the same approach, don't you?"

"Let me go, Haynes," Chalyce commanded, trying to appear unruffled. "This is not amusing."

Haynes chuckled. "It is not meant to be amusing, Chalyce," he said, moving to kiss her.

Chalyce leaned away from him, but she could not pull her arms from his tightening grip.

"Let go of me!" she cried. "He did not deliver me from the Cochrans to place me into your hands!"

"No, he did not. You are right about that, Chalyce," he said. "We both know why he brought you here, now don't we? Race Trevelian is not as pure as the driven snow, you realize. I am certain he has plans for you…or perhaps you already know what his plans were."

"He has not touched me."

"That's a lie, and you know it!"

"He hasn't! Not since that night, weeks ago!" she assured him, struggling.

"He is just biding his time, Chalyce…until he's had his fill of Helena Dickson."

At that moment, the smokehouse door burst open to reveal an enraged Race Trevelian.

"You!" Race growled through clenched teeth as he took hold of Haynes's coat collar.

Race wrenched the man from the smokehouse and planted a fist squarely in his face. Haynes fell to the ground—his nose misshapen and bleeding.

"What is it, Trevelian?" Haynes asked, sitting up and dabbing at his bloodied face with one hand. "Too selfish to share the spoils? You want her all to yourself, is that it?"

Reaching down and taking hold of Haynes's coat lapels, Race jerked him to his feet.

Drawing back a fist and making ready to inflict another blow upon the man, Race said, "You are going to bleed for this, Haynes."

Before he could administer the punch, however, Chalyce moved to take his powerful fist between her own hands.

"Don't, Race," she said. "Let it go."

Race looked to her in disgusted disbelief. "You're defending him?" he asked.

"He was your friend not a moment ago," she reminded the infuriated man.

Drawing a deep breath, Race pushed Haynes to the ground and stormed away.

"I cannot believe it," Haynes mused, dabbing once more at his face. "You probably just saved my life."

Chalyce nodded as she watched Race disappear into the house, slamming the door behind him.

"Yes," she breathed. "But I did it for his sake...not for yours."

❧

"Will he leave, Lyle?" Chalyce asked as she and Lyle sat alone in the library that evening.

"How can he?" Lyle mumbled, shaking his head. "Haynes has nowhere to go...even if he could get off the mountain."

Chalyce wondered how Haynes could continue working and residing under the same roof after such a confrontation with his employer. Yet as she stared out through the window into the frigid winter's evening, her thoughts turned again to Race.

"Is he in love with her, Lyle?" she asked.

"Who?" Lyle inquired.

"This Helena Dickson. Is Race in love with her?"

Lyle burst into laughter. "What? Race? In love with Helena? How could you ever conjure such an absurd notion, Chalyce?"

Chalyce glanced away, blushing with humiliation.

"Oh. I see," Lyle said as understanding washed over him. "No, Chalyce. I assure you love is the furthest emotion from Race's heart where Helena Dickson is concerned."

"Then why?" she asked. "Why does he go, month after month? He spends nearly the entire night there. What else could transpire between them if not...?"

Lyle stood and walked to where Chalyce stood, joining her in gazing out through the window.

"Imagine yourself on the outside, Chalyce," he began. "Out there...looking in...the cold silence all about you...nothing but the cold and silence. You press your face to the icy glass, trying to feel the warmth burning from the fire within...but there only comes a stinging pain...the only thing the cold, lifeless glass can give to you as you stand in the frozen silence. And so rather than stare at what you think you cannot have, you remain standing in the cold, black emptiness."

"You are telling me that he is afraid to warm himself, Lyle? Is that what you're saying?" Chalyce sighed with impatience. "Race Trevelian is not afraid of anything, and you know it better than I do."

"Indeed, I do, Chalyce. Yet everyone harbors a secret...a tragic moment...an intense fear that tragedy will find them again. Some pick up and move on. Others...it nearly breaks their spirit. Guilt and anguish never abandon them," he explained.

"Then what is it? Tell me, Lyle," Chalyce pleaded.

"Look…he's returning!" Lyle mumbled. A sudden expression of something akin to panic caused his brow to furrow. "Quickly! To bed with you, Chalyce. He will be in a nasty temper tonight."

She quickly dashed up the stairs and into her room just as she heard the angry march of Race's boots in the entryway.

"All is the same?" she heard Lyle ask, just as he did upon each of Race's returns.

"Precisely," echoed Race's familiar response.

Hours and hours later, Chalyce was still unable to fall to sleep. She thought perhaps seeking out something warm or sweet from the kitchen might help to induce a relaxation to her mind and body. Perhaps a glass of warmed milk and a piece of the cake Haynes had served after dinner.

As she passed the library on her way to the kitchen, however, her ears caught the faint sound of a distressed moaning. The library door stood open, and a fire blazed in the hearth. There, as ever—in a chair before the fire—sat Race. The moaning seemed to emanate from him, and Chalyce's curiosity overruled her good sense as she quietly slipped into the room.

At first she thought he was awake, for from her position at his back she could see that his hands gripped the arms of the chair so tightly as to cause them to be pale and trembling. As he again groaned, she stepped to his side to see that his eyes were, indeed, closed.

"Mr. Trevelian?" she whispered. His eyes remained closed, but he wore a painful grimace on his face. Perspiration beaded on his forehead, trickling over his brow and temples.

Chalyce knelt before him, gazing up into the face contorted with anguish.

"Mr. Trevelian?" she ventured once more. His shirt hung open, and she could see that every muscle revealed was tensed. His legs were tensed as well, pushing his body back against the chair. He was obviously enduring a nightmare.

"Mr. Trevelian? Race?" she said, gently laying her hand on his leg.

Race gasped as his eyes burst open, releasing one tear to travel over his cheek. He blinked to clear his vision.

"What are you doing?" he asked, his voice quaking with emotion.

"You were dreaming." Chalyce watched in wonder as his hands, still trembling, went to his face. He wiped the moisture from his brow—and cheeks. "Are you well?" she asked, concerned for his well-being.

He looked at her, shaking his head and chuckling—and she wondered at the state of his sanity.

"Am I fine?" he repeated. "No, Chalyce…I am diseased. Diseased of mind…and that condition causes a pestilence of my very being!"

His entire body trembled so violently that the feminine instinct to nurture caused Chalyce to reach out and take one of his hands reassuringly in her own.

"You're so pale," she said in a whisper. "What is it that so plagues your thoughts? What causes you to be cruel…to dream dreams so horrific that a body as powerful as yours quakes?"

Race raised his free hand to his eyes and studied it as it trembled before him. "It is the sound too, you understand," he began, "but most of all the taste of it. I cannot rid my memory of the taste of it."

"The taste of what?" she asked. "What lamentable memory eats at your mind, Race?"

He wiped his lips with the back of his hand, as if trying to rid his mouth of some repugnant flavor.

"It's the taste most of all," he repeated—more to himself than to Chalyce. "I have tasted it every day since, except when…"

It was then Chalyce began to tremble—for the look in his eyes as he gazed at her was wildly unsettling. Her body was frozen to the spot before him—unmoving—so that even as he reached out, gently taking her face in his trembling hands, she could not move.

"Did you taste it?" he asked. "That day out by the woodpile when I kissed you…did you taste it?"

"What?" she breathed—for she had never known such a perplexing moment.

"That was the first time in seemingly endless years that the vile flavor of it was driven from my mouth. It was as if I had been dining forever on nothing but bitter, rancid meat…and then suddenly being given a succulent bowl of sweet cherries…sun-ripened and fresh from the tree." He bent toward her until his face was exactly in front of hers. "Help me now, Chalyce," he breathed. "Do not deny me that coveted refreshment. Renew it once more…if only for a moment."

His alluring features and enthralling words mesmerized Chalyce. He appeared so honest—so forthright in that moment. She felt she was blessed with a glimpse into the true soul hiding beneath the physical shell of the man. Her heart cried out to her mind then, begging that her consciousness accept and admit what her essence had known all along: she loved him! She was wholly and everlastingly in love with Race Trevelian!

As his quivering lips brushed her own, she made no move to escape. She could feel his entire being trembling as he slid from the chair, dropping to his knees before her and gathering her into his powerful arms. His lips parted as he kissed her again, coaxing her to join him in a shared and deeply intimate emotional exchange. As the welcome sensation of euphoria induced by his touch blissfully drowned her, Chalyce found herself defenseless and unable to fathom the desire to flee from him.

She could feel the anguished pain leaving his body as he slowly ceased trembling. His kisses became more sure—more demanding—and the strength and power that was him returned. With a heavy sigh, he instructed her in one last fiery, impassioned kiss before he tenderly cupped her chin in one hand, smiling at her.

"You are purely medicinal, Chalyce...but I am beyond healing," he said. He released her and stood. "Yet fear not. I will not taint your innocence of experience and peaceful conscience any further this night." She stood, opening her mouth to speak in his defense, but he raised an index finger and cocked his head to one side, stalling her. "I do thank you for awakening me. I was steeped in a most unpleasant...recollection. I am a beast to have used you in such a manner. And I assure...I did use you. I make you the offer once more, brat. Stay with me here this night. I guarantee that the remainder of winter would pass more pleasantly for the both of us if you do."

Chalyce's eyes narrowed as she studied his expression, or rather his lack of expression. She reached up and laid one hand against his warm, unshaven cheek. Instantly he pulled away from her touch, and she smiled with triumph.

"You have tipped your hand too far this night, Race Trevelian...and in your own favor," she said. "You would never take any woman to your bed save she was your legally wed wife...and I know it now. I shall no longer be moved at your threats of violating me, for I know you would never do such a thing. I have seen into the very deepest abyss of your soul this night."

"Then you have seen the devil there…and you know what I am capable of," he growled, turning from her and storming out of the room.

# CHAPTER FIVE

"There is nothing amiss, Lyle," Chalyce heard Race say.

She hesitated before entering the kitchen for breakfast, scolding herself for pampering such a profoundly bad habit as eavesdropping.

"I have simply slept well for once and am in a quite good-humored frame of mind," Race concluded.

"I have never seen you thus after an evening with Helena," Lyle noted.

"Helena has nothing whatsoever to do with it," Race informed the man. "I may even be able to tolerate Haynes's ugly mug this morning."

"I'm to thank you for that comment, I suppose," Haynes muttered.

"Sleeping in a bed is much preferable to that blasted chair, I will give you that," Race said. "Chairs are nightmarish pieces of furniture. But a bed...now therein is comfort...and I've Chalyce to thank for that."

Chalyce ceased her eavesdropping and burst into the room when she heard the crashing of plates and chairs. Gasping, she found herself witness to the aftermath of an act of violence.

Race lay on the floor, his chair tipped over and several plates smashed and lying about in pieces around him. He was rubbing his jaw, and Haynes stood looming angrily over him.

Haynes looked up to Chalyce—the rage all too apparent in his face.

"So it is what I thought, isn't it?" he growled. "He is the king of the mountain, and that is what you wanted."

"What are you talking about, Haynes?" Chalyce exclaimed. "I only woke him from a bad dream! That is what he's referring to!"

"Woke him from a bad dream, is it? Oh, I have no doubt of that," Haynes spat.

Chalyce watched as Race slowly stood. Straightening his collar, he said in a calm voice,

"Forgive me, Haynes. You misunderstood me." Then turning to Chalyce, he asked, "May I speak to you privately in the library for a moment?"

Chalyce followed in silence, still disturbed at what had transpired in the kitchen.

Race closed the library door and began, "I have asked you in here to offer my sincerest apologies for…for my behavior on several occasions since your arrival."

Chalyce frowned. "Haynes only this moment belted your jaw! Aren't you angry with him?" she asked.

"I should have chosen my words more carefully," Race explained. "But, again, this is not the subject that I wish to discuss with you." His gaze never left hers for a moment as he continued. "I have behaved appallingly toward you while you have been here. I am a frightful human being, and I suppose that can account for it…at least, part of it. I'm a private man, and I viewed you as an intruder to my solitude. However, I admit now that this was no fault of yours. You and I are merely victims of the irrational endeavors of the loathsome Cochran family. Therefore, I truly ask that you pardon me for my somewhat iniquitous behavior at times."

Chalyce raised her brows in skepticism.

"Ah, I see that you doubt the sincerity of my repentance," Race chuckled. "I would remind you that I am not promising I will act only affably and with great etiquette at all times...only that I realize my error in my treatment of you thus far."

"Thank you...I-I suppose," Chalyce stammered.

Race nodded and reached to open the door, thus signaling the conclusion of their conversation.

"Just a moment, if you please," Chalyce began quickly. As Race paused and looked to her once more, she said, "I would like to ask you about—"

"You will kindly refrain from the asking, Chalyce," he interrupted.

"But last night...I think I deserve—"

"I thank you wholeheartedly for your administering to me such a vastly needed solace. But divulging any further explanation to you is unthinkable. Do not ask about it again, Chalyce." He opened the door, but before exiting, he turned to her once more, adding, "One thing more...you are a guest in this house. As such, it is time you were treated as one. Your time is your own. Enjoy the remaining winter months as you will. I will inform Lyle that he may cease inventing chores for you."

❧

"You see...you have touched him," Lyle remarked as Chalyce sat with him that evening in the kitchen. "Race Trevelian is not the ogre you thought him to be, is he?"

"You know I never thought him an ogre," Chalyce muttered.

"It is well I do know it...and well I understand why you tried to convince yourself of it."

"What do you mean by that?" she asked with rising indignation.

"Race Trevelian has always fascinated women," Lyle explained. "They are drawn to him like bees to apple blossoms."

"Are you insinuating that I...I am not attracted to him!" Chalyce lied.

Lyle seemed to ignore her and continued, "Even Helena Dickson. I tried to tell him that she had a hand in...but he does not see it, and she holds the reins of guilt tightly around his throat."

"Lyle," Chalyce ventured, "please tell me whatever it is you all hide for him."

Again Lyle continued, seeming to ignore her. "What a congenial fellow he was before," he chuckled. "Always involved in some sort of horseplay or teasing. And generous he was…near to a fault." Lyle looked at Chalyce, his eyes burning with a bright intensity. "You have seen it in him, have you not?" he asked.

"What do you mean?" Chalyce mumbled, glancing away—blushing.

"You have seen into his soul, Chalyce. You know the man who lurks beneath the granite sculpture."

Chalyce looked up to Lyle once more. "Tell me, Lyle. Please tell me," she pleaded.

"The horror is not mine to tell, Chalyce," he said. "But remember, patience often affords a prize, my dear. Be patient, Chalyce. You have touched him. Now, be patient."

Chalyce sighed—drank from her cup of hot, nutmegged milk. She wondered why Lyle must forever and always talk in riddles. And "horror," he had said. What was the horror he could not tell?

# CHAPTER SIX

"Good morning, all!" Race greeted as he entered the kitchen one cold December morning. He put his hands to his chest and inhaled deeply, exhaling the breath with a satisfied, "Aaahhh." He continued, "The air is fragrant with the scent of cinnamon this morning, Haynes. And I am ravenous as well as cheerful."

As he sat down next to her, Chalyce arched one brow in astonishment at his good-natured attitude.

"What? Do my radiant good looks unsettle you this fine winter's morn, Chalyce?" he teased.

"Nothing about you unsettles me, sir," Chalyce sighed, feigning indifference.

"Nothing, you say? Well, then I will have to try harder if I'm to capture your interest, I suppose," he chuckled. "What say you to a ride this afternoon,

Lyle? We've not been out in days. The sun is bright, and I sense the weather may accommodate us."

"That would excellent, sir," Lyle answered.

"You are more than welcome to join us if you like, Chalyce," Race said as he began heartily devouring his breakfast.

"Thank you, sir...but I do not have appropriate attire for such an excursion," she reminded him.

"Nonsense, Chalyce!" Race exclaimed. "Just after breakfast we'll run up to my room and try some of my things on you. I'm certain we can squeeze you into a pair of my trousers."

"Oh, you are quite certain, are you?" Chalyce asked with sarcasm. "I would not want my rotund form splitting out your seams."

Race smiled. "There is nothing rotund about your scant little figure, Chalyce."

"What do you mean by that?" Chalyce asked, somewhat offended.

"My, my, Lyle...I think we have stumbled onto a sensitive subject where Miss LaSalle is concerned," he mumbled.

"I am not afraid, if that is what you think," Chalyce stated. "I can ride with the best horseman! And I am not averse to wearing your trousers either. I would be overjoyed to breathe some fresh air. It seems a little stale in here." She shoved her chair away from the table, rose, and left. Chalyce smiled, however, when she heard Race and Lyle chuckling together. She had seen the change in him over the past few days. He had even begun to sleep in his bedchamber more often than not.

"Very well, see if these will do for you," Race said, handing her a pair of trousers and a shirt. "The trousers were in a trunk. I wore them when I was fourteen. They are the smallest pair I could find. You will simply have to endure the overabundance of the shirt." He chuckled, adding, "It is, however, lacking yolk and grease stains."

"Thank you," Chalyce said, smiling sweetly as she shut the door to her bedchamber pointedly in his face.

After she had removed her dress (which had become far more than well-worn from her wearing it every day and washing it so often), she put on the shirt Race had given her. Immediately an odd sense of indulging in some sort of improper intimacy washed over her. The feeling of having cloth that had been worn by him caressing her own skin sent her senses spinning. She lifted one shoulder and let her face nuzzle the fabric—taking in the faint aroma of shaving soap and cedar smoke. Yes, it was familiar—too familiar. Chalyce shook her head, trying to dispel the memories of his kisses—for whether heartlessly administered or tender, Race Trevelian's kisses were the stuff of heaven! Yet the visions of those occasions when she had been held in his arms while he favored her mouth with the taste of his own dominated visions in her mind.

As she quickly pulled on the trousers he had given her, she brushed a betraying tear from her cheeks.

"Stop, Chalyce," she scolded herself. "He is…he is…not for you. Most likely demented in some way as well."

Still, when she studied herself in the mirror before leaving her room, the explosive thrill filling her for the sake of the knowledge that she wore his clothes caused goose bumps to race over her body.

"Stop," she muttered to herself as she went to her door and opened it.

The goose bumps blanketing her flesh only increased in their prickling when she saw Race stood directly before her—his arms folded across his broad chest. He had obviously waited the entire time she was changing.

"Well, now…they will do, will they not?" he asked as he inspected her from head to toe. "Yes," he mumbled, taking a step forward, thereby crossing the threshold to her room. "My clothes seem to hide that curvaceous little frame of yours very thoroughly." Smiling and in a lowered voice, he added, "Blasted thoroughly."

Chalyce gasped as he then reached out, pulling her to him. Her infinite thirst for his kiss knew a measure of quenching as the warmth of his mouth melded with her own.

"You are the heaven-sent cure for the disease that eats away at me, are you not?" he whispered, breaking their kiss and gently cradling her face in one hand as he gazed into her eyes.

"You said you would not…" she began—breathless.

Race put an index finger to her lips, silencing her words.

"I apologized for my previous behavior," he said. "I never said that I would not kiss you again."

"You are cruel to toy with people so," Chalyce said, pushing herself from his arms.

"I have never toyed with anyone in my life, Chalyce!" he growled. "Not even..." Yet he broke off and inhaled a deep, calming breath. "Come now. Have you ever ridden in snow this deep? It is quite exhilarating."

Then taking her hand, he led her to the coat closet where he removed one of his enormous coats and helped her into it.

The frigid winter air stung Chalyce's face, and she owned the sensation that her nose was constantly dripping. Still, Race had been correct; it did indeed feel wonderful to be out in the fresh air. They would not go far on horseback, no doubt—for the snow was deep, making progression slow and strenuous for their mounts.

"Is it not breathtaking in its silence, Chalyce?" Lyle inquired.

Chalyce had noticed the silence in the wood—not a bird chirping, not a scampering fox or mouse to be seen.

"Yes," she agreed. "Yet almost eerie."

The three rode on, speaking little, thus simply enjoying the outing.

Then, just before they were to turn back, another rider approached.

Chalyce knew at once who the rider was, even before she was clearly visible. As Helena Dickson reined in next to Race, Chalyce's stomach churned with ominous trepidation.

"Oh, Race!" the beautiful, fair-haired woman panted. She was obviously distressed, and somehow her features were even lovelier for the sake of it. "Race, darling! How relieved I am to have found you! They told me at the house that you were out riding, and I simply knew I would not find you in time!"

"Helena," Race greeted—though with an expression of loathing Chalyce did not expect. "Whatever has you in such a twist this time?"

When Chalyce looked from Race back to the waiting woman, it was in time to see the woman glaring her with seething resentment. The expression passed from her face quickly, however.

"Who is this, Race?" Helena asked. "I do not believe you mentioned to me you had hired a girl to help keep your house."

"This is Chalyce LaSalle, Helena…and she is not an employee of mine. Rather she is my—" Race began.

"Very well, Race," Helena interrupted. "However, if you felt you were in need of a woman's care…you know I would willingly have—"

"What has you so excitable, Helena?" Race growled. "For pity's sake, woman! You come riding in with a thistle under your saddle and then stop to chat about—"

"It is those awful Cochrans, Race! They have abducted my Cynthia! My very own employee! You know Cynthia. She is the one you send into fits of blushing each time you—"

"Yes, yes, Helena," Race grumbled. He frowned. "The Cochrans, is it? I am not surprised." He turned to Lyle. "Lyle, take Chalyce and Helena back to the house," he ordered. "Then have Haynes, Peter, and Marcus join us in the search. I will begin now."

Something in the very depths of Chalyce's soul shrieked out in warning. So strongly did it echo in her mind that she reached out, taking hold of Race's coat sleeve.

"Please wait for the others," she pleaded.

"I will be fine. There has not been a Cochran born yet that could take me in a fight," he said. His mount reared, and he rode away.

"Please go with him, Lyle," Chalyce pleaded. "Something is not right."

"Of course something is not right, girl!" Helena spat. "Cynthia has been abducted! And by those vile Cochran brothers. You of all people should know how that feels!"

"Come along, Chalyce," Lyle said, looking to Helena with suspicion. "I will join him as soon as you are safe."

Yet as Chalyce watched from the library window as Lyle rode off into the winter dusk, the sickening anxiety within her only boiled. Something was terribly wrong—and she knew it with every strand of her being. She stood for nearly an hour at the window— watching—waiting. At last, Helena's syrupy voice drew her from her thoughts.

"They will be well, if that is why you are keeping a vigil at that window," Helena said.

Chalyce turned and looked to the woman. Yes— she was quite beautiful. She boasted golden hair and the bluest eyes. Her figure was perfect and her lips a ripe cherry red. Still, Chalyce saw something beneath the outer beauty. At that moment, Lyle's words concerning Race came into her mind like a detonation of realization.

*You know the man who lurks beneath the granite sculpture*, he had said.

And as Chalyce looked now into the eyes of Helena Dickson, Lyle's words held a different meaning. The question came into her mind, *What woman lurks beneath the flawless beauty before me?*

"Race had not mentioned my being here to you?" Chalyce asked.

"No," Helena answered. "Perhaps he thought I might become jealous if I knew he were sheltering a woman under his roof. But now that I have seen you…he truly had no cause to keep it from me."

"Yet you knew, Helena," Chalyce said. "You knew of my abduction at the hand of the Cochran brothers."

Helena shifted in her chair. "I had heard of it from another source."

"The only other source on the mountain in winter is the Cochran family."

"What are you implying, girl?" Helena growled, jumping to her feet and stomping one foot.

Chalyce's attention was arrested at that moment, however, by a loud neighing and pounding of horse hooves outside. Quickly, she turned back to the window, gasping at the sight of Race's riderless horse.

"His horse!" she cried, turning to face Helena again. "His horse has returned without him!"

"Without him?" Helena gasped—though obviously feigning her horror.

"Get out!" Chalyce cried. "Get out of his house this minute!"

Helena frowned—appeared astonished by Chalyce's demand. "What do you mean, girl?" she asked. "Race sent me here."

"And you sent him on an imagined errand! I do not know what he hides or what you hide, for that matter...but get out!" Going to where the woman stood, Chalyce grabbed a handful of her hair and began pulling her toward the front door.

"Do not meddle with me, girl!" Helena shrieked. "It will be on peril of your life!"

Chalyce pushed her through the front door, slamming it in her face.

Quickly then she put on the coat Race had covered her with earlier and left the house by way of the kitchen. With great courage, she approached the riderless horse and took hold of the bit.

"Whoa, boy. You settle down now," she soothed. "I need your help."

The horse settled and allowed Chalyce to mount him. Snow was falling heavily now, and she nearly gave in to panic when she realized she had no idea in which direction to search. Yet slowly the horse began to move forward—and she could only pray he would take her back to his master.

It seemed an unendurable eternity before Race's horse finally stopped at a small clearing some ways from the house. Chalyce slid from the animal's back—kneeling in the snow next to a bruised and broken body of Race Trevelian.

Tears filled her eyes, for she thought him surely dead. His shirt was torn completely from his body and—laying nearby—wet with blood. He lay in the snow on his back, and the brutal bruising to his face and ribs was already so vividly purple that Chalyce's own flesh ached upon witnessing it. His chin and one cheek were simply covered with drying blood emanating from inside his mouth. There was a severe laceration on his forehead just at his hairline, and the blood from it had caked to his left brow.

Gently she took one of his powerful hands in her own and quickly studied it. The knuckles of the hand she held, as well as the other, were torn and bleeding. Race Trevelian had truly fought for his life! The wisps of his breath manifest in the air were proof he lived still, and Chalyce spoke softly to him as her tears fell upon his bruised and bloodied chest.

"Race?" she whispered at first. "Oh please, Race," she pleaded. "You have to wake. I cannot possibly manage to get you to the house otherwise."

There came a pained moan from deep within his throat as his eyes opened and he looked at her. Relief flooded Chalyce as she gazed into the brilliance of his still-smoldering green eyes.

"Can you move, sir?" she asked. "We must get home somehow."

He tried to sit but winced at the pain the effort caused.

"I can help you," Chalyce said. Quickly she removed the coat she wore, placing it about his broad shoulders. Taking hold of both his arms, she pulled with every ounce of strength left in her shivering body. With the little aid Race could give her, they were able to pull him to a sitting position.

"Stand now," she ordered. Drawing a deep breath, Race forced himself to his feet with her assistance—falling against her several times before gaining his own balance.

"You have to mount your horse, Race. Do you hear me?" she cried. She could see he was weak and near to falling unconscious. "Mount that horse!" she ordered.

She knew every breath pained him and that his body must be numb from the cold. Yet with great strength and effort he mounted. Once mounted securely in front of him, she urged the horse forward. Race's great form slumped against her—the weight of him almost overwhelming. Still, Chalyce knew his only chance at survival was to return home to shelter. Lyle would have returned and would be able to help them.

The storm was turning violent by the time the lights from the windows of the house beckoned to Chalyce. She hoped Helena did not know she had left and returned to the house. She had barely enough strength to assist Race. There would be none left to deal with the witch.

Somehow Chalyce managed to help Race down from the horse and into the house. Quickly she stoked the dying fire in the library hearth and laid him on the soft, white rug before it.

"Warm him first," she mumbled to herself. Going to the kitchen, she removed the kettle from the stove and returned to the library.

"Lyle!" she called—frantic. "Haynes?"

There came no reply. No one had returned from the search. There was no time to cry—no time to melt into frightened sobbing. Thus, she forced back the tears that threatened to break her. Grabbing for a discarded shirt lying in the big chair (no doubt abandoned by Race the previous night), she ignored the uncomfortable cold in her own hands and spread the shirt over Race's torso and arms.

As she studied his battered face, her tears did escape then—for the wounds and dried blood were a painful sight. Frantically, she tugged at the tail of the shirt she wore, dampening it with the kettle water.

The blood came away from his face fairly easily, but she was startled when she saw the blue tinge of his lips. She felt his face; he was still dangerously cold. Moving to his feet, she tugged at his boots until they slipped off. Removing his stockings, she found his feet were cold and bluing as well.

Snatching a quilt from the nearby sofa, she placed it over his lower body. She added wood to the fire until it was blazing hot and almost unbearable for her. Chalyce removed the shirt from his torso and held it close to the flames, placing it over him once more when it had warmed. Still, his lips were blue, and he remained unconscious.

"Race, please," she pleaded, smoothing his hair as she spoke to him.

He opened his eyes to narrow slits and mumbled, "It's blasted cold in here, Chalyce."

Smiling as hope filled her bosom, she nodded. "Yes, it is," she agreed, noticing goose bumps were appearing over his exposed flesh. It was a good indication.

He managed to sit up. "A warm drink would help, I think," he mumbled.

"Yes, of course," Chalyce agreed, jumping to her feet and dashing to the kitchen.

When he had finished the drink, Race was quite alert—though in great pain.

"She sent you out with the intent you would come to harm, Race," Chalyce told him as she began to feel confident he would be well. "She had you ambushed...I have no doubt of it."

"It was the Cochran brothers...all four of them," he said. "No doubt they are still miffed about my spoiling their plans where you are concerned. Still, I gave a good accounting of myself." He paused a moment—grew pallid and exclaimed, "Cynthia! Did anyone find her?"

"Cynthia?" Chalyce asked. "Sir...I am certain Cynthia is well and fine. Did you not hear me? I am telling you that Helena planned for the Cochrans to attack you!"

"Helena?" Race asked, frowning. "Why would Helena want harm to come to me? I do everything for her."

"I do not know, sir...but she did. In my soul I know she did," Chalyce said.

Chalyce watched as Race was silent for a moment. His gaze drifted past her to a space beyond.

"Melisia was Helena's sister...her elder sister," he said at last.

"What?" Chalyce asked, bewildered.

"Helena's sister...Melisia," he breathed.

Assuming he had endured one too many blows to the head, Chalyce decided to allow him to babble while she tended his wounds. However, his next utterance captivated her attention entirely.

"Melisia and I were…courting, I suppose you would call it." The look of doubt on Chalyce's face seemed to prompt him further. "Yes, brat…I have been known to pay court to beautiful young ladies…though not as of late." He lay back on the rug, grimacing and putting a hand to his badly bruised ribs.

"I am sure they are completely broken up inside," Chalyce interjected, gesturing to his rib cage.

"No. Just battered a bit," he breathed. "Now, do you want me to tell you or not? Do you want to know what a vile and loathsome creature you are attending to? Do you want to know why Helena would send me to my death, Chalyce?"

"Yes," she affirmed—though she was not at all sure she did want to know. Until that moment, the secret may have been her own imagination. But now it would be real—and it involved Helena.

"I had been visiting Melisia, somewhat lightheartedly, for several months," he began. "This was near to four years past, you understand. Unbeknownst to me, however, Melisia—in her own mind—saw things as very serious indeed…to a point that she was anticipating a proposal from me. I was vain…perhaps even naive…plain brainless…and did not sense the depth of her infatuation with me. One day, Helena tried to warn me. She insisted that her sister was blindly in love with me and a very frail, emotional girl...that I should take care not to upset her. I assured Helena that I had no serious intentions toward her sister, and for some sadistic reason that I have never been able to discern, Helena went to Melisia and informed her of my dalliance."

"She was jealous," Chalyce muttered.

"What?" he asked, looking to her. "Jealousy? No. Spiteful, perhaps...but not jealous."

Chalyce remained silent—for she could not believe he was truly unaware of the obvious passions driving Helena.

"It was late that same evening," he continued, "and Lyle came to my chambers to inform me that Melisia was calling. 'At this hour?' I asked. Yet I went down to meet her, and as I began to inquire as to the reason for her untimely visit, she pulled from beneath her cloak a pistol. She leveled it and shot me in the left thigh."

"What?" Chalyce gasped—for she had not expected such a revelation. "Melisia shot you? You? The man she was in love with?"

Race nodded and closed his eyes for a moment before sitting up and continuing. His eyes burned into Chalyce's as resentment and guilt filled them.

"I was so astonished, my knees weakened, and I fell to the floor," he explained. "Melisia rushed to me…tears streaming down her lovely cheeks. I was stunned to silence at first. She said she was sorry…that she loved me…and that if she could not possess me, no one would. She meant to murder me then, you see." He spoke with such unsettling plainness it caused the hair on the back of Chalyce's neck to prickle.

"Surely you are only trying to frighten me," Chalyce mumbled in disbelieving astonishment. "Surely this cannot be true."

"Do you think Helena would bother with me if it were a mere fairy tale, Chalyce?" he growled. "I was lying thus," he nearly shouted as he reached forward, taking hold of her arm and pulling her back fiercely until she lay flat on the rug next to him. "The wound had shocked me, rendered me speechless. Lyle was just coming down the stairs. Melisia came to sit next to me, like so," he growled, raising himself on one elbow and bending over Chalyce. "She had removed a second pistol from her cloak and put the gun to my temple." He pressed one index finger against her temple. "Then, she put her mouth to mine. 'The kiss of death,' I remember thinking. I was too stunned…still paralyzed with unbelieving. 'The kiss of death,' I thought again…and that, my innocent dove, is exactly what it was."

Chalyce stared into the fiery jade of his eyes as they flashed with the pain and anger of the memory.

Race tenderly brushed the hair from her face and continued in a whisper, "I watched as Melisia drew the gun from my own head and placed it at the top of hers, like so." Still using his finger to indicate the position of the pistol barrel, he placed it at the top of his head just above his forehead so that it pointed downward. "She looked into my eyes once more and said, 'I love you, Race. I could never kill you…but I cannot live without your love.' Then she kissed me again…and with her mouth opened and pressed to mine…she pulled the trigger." His mouth captured Chalyce's in a hot, moist kiss. "Bang!" he exclaimed suddenly, causing her to gasp. "The bullet shot down through her head…through the roof of her mouth…exited through the back of her neck. Her blood and tissue began spilling into my mouth. It quickly covered my face and saturated my shirt," he breathed, rolling away from Chalyce and onto his back once more.

"I-I am so sorry," Chalyce wept, brushing the tears from her cheeks. What more could be said in response to such an account? Closing her eyes, she tried to dispel the gruesome vision forming in her mind. "W-why would she be so cruel to you?" she stammered. "She was in love with you! Why would she want to hurt you?"

Race closed his own eyes. "Helena blamed me...and she was right to," he says.

"But it was not your fault," Chalyce defended. "The woman was...mad...obsessed." She sat up, her tears increasing as she looked to him—so filled with guilt, anguish, and misery.

"I should have seen it," he mumbled, "but I didn't. People are weak. I learned that then. Far better it is to harden oneself...sympathize with no one. Thus, I am now the man you see lying next to you...uncaring, hardened, cruel...as I should be. And all was well...until the fateful day the loathsome Cochrans took it into their tiny brains to spirit you away from your family to cross my path."

He opened his eyes—glared at her with bitter resentment.

"Me?" she exclaimed. "I have done nothing to you!"

"Oh, haven't you?" he growled. "You in constant threaten to breach my defenses at every turn!"

"How?" she asked, brushing at her tears again.

"By existing here!" he rumbled. "By waltzing out to the smokehouse one day to come upon me splitting wood."

Chalyce blushed at the memory. "I do not see what that has to do with—"

" 'You really should dress properly for the cold, you know'," Race said, imitating her feminine voice.

"What do you imply?" she demanded. "I was truly concerned for your well-being!"

"I thought to myself, *I'll kiss the little chit. One taste of her and that bloody remembrance will fill my mouth again.* But you thwarted me, did you not?"

Chalyce shook her head. "What are you talking about? I have done nothing to—"

"And so I did. I roughly took your rose-petal lips with my indifferent ones…and to what end? I will tell you, Chalyce. It was an unsought purification! All that I had worked to become…every feeling I had buried burst to the surface, threatening to undo me. For the memory of Melisia did not return as I expected…did not interfere with the refreshment I drew from you. I knew how dangerous you were to me then...how capable you were of destroying me. I have fallen into your snare more than once, have I not?"

"Me?" she gasped. "Me? I am not the one who put a pistol to my head and...and...you have a very distorted perception of danger, Mr. Trevelian." She stood and began pacing angrily in front of him. "I am not the one who sent you to your assured death this very night either! How selfish! Playing the martyr as it were...by barring yourself from the world. Such vanity!" she raged. "What? Did you assume that every woman on earth would shoot her head open at the thought of not possessing you? And what utter stupidity!" He stood—weak yet drawing angry breath—facing her as she continued. "What do you think Helena intended when she told Melisia? She knew her sister better than anyone! No doubt Helena knew just how her sister would react should she find out that you had no loving regard for her! Why do you think she took it upon herself to inform her sister of your feelings? Well, I will tell you...for you are obviously too dimwitted to have seen it for yourself. Helena was and is in love with you, Race! To the point of wishing death upon her own sister! And now—now that she knows there is no chance of your ever returning her passions—she took the same road her sister did…only taking the opposite venue at the fork. Instead of killing herself…she determined to kill you!"

"You are insane, Chalyce," he growled. "Helena? Send her own sister to her death? You are mad."

Chalyce shook her head. "Do not deny it, Race. You were wretched enough to be the unwilling participant in a malevolent love triangle…with two demented sisters at the helm. And do not blame me for thwarting your efforts at being the sadistic recluse! Any man of your age and…depth of masculinity who had kept himself from female companionship would find me enticing, I suppose. Do not blame me for being the subject at hand during your weak moment!" she spat.

He collapsed to his hands and knees—defeated. "You are wrong," he mumbled, weary from breathing and verbal battle. "It was you. No other woman…only you could have…"

"Don't you see?" Chalyce asked, dropping to her knees beside him. Her anger had dissipated instantly. She knew and understood that he had been the victim in the catastrophe. She had no right to be so angry with him. He had only lashed at her for the sake of his fatigue and overwhelming guilt. "It was not your fault. She was the villain, Race. Not you."

Race lay down once more and closed his eyes. "You are wrong about Helena, Chalyce," he sighed. "Otherwise…she would have attempted to rid me of you…instead of me."

Chalyce shivered even though the fire made the room almost uncomfortably hot. "That venue failed to win you before, Race."

"I am weary, Chalyce," he breathed. "Tired and beaten, and my mind is a void. Go to sleep. The others will return soon, and the storm will more likely than not have cleared by morning." Reaching out, he took hold of her wrist and tugged at it. "Now, lie down here and rest with me. Your wakefulness will disturb my sleep."

Chalyce did lie down next to him.

"Such drastic lengths you have put me through, Chalyce…in order to finally have you where I want you," he chuckled.

Chalyce made no reprimanding remark—for his breathing indicated he was already asleep and would not hear her.

# CHAPTER SEVEN

Lyle and the others did indeed return, and Chalyce was grateful. Race, however, was ill and feverish for several days as a result of the incident.

"The snow is still too deep for me to ride over and confront her, Chalyce," Lyle explained at breakfast the fourth day following Race's confrontation with the Cochrans. "The storm was merciless in its fury."

"Good. Maybe she froze out in it," Chalyce mumbled. "Maybe she's lying stiff and dead under a tree somewhere." Chalyce pondered the thought only for a moment—for even though the woman was capable of atrocity, she would not wish to be responsible for Helena's death. "Do you think I should have thrown her out, Lyle? I mean, I really had no authority to act so—"

"I might have done worse, Chalyce," Lyle assured her. "I tried to convince Race of her deceitful, conniving ways...but he would not accept it."

"You falsely accuse Helena. Both of you," Haynes suddenly growled. He pointed to Lyle, saying, "You because you are so blindly loyal to Trevelian!" Pointing to Chalyce, he said, "And you...you because you are so blindly in love with him!"

"We are not blind, Haynes!" Chalyce defended herself and Lyle. "She is mad! It is obvious in her very demeanor. And what reason do you have to turncoat on Race?"

"Because I knew Melisia Dickson, Chalyce," he growled, leveling his face with her own. "She was an innocent! A beautiful, delicate innocent! Race Trevelian encouraged her feelings for him...led her to believe he cared for her...toyed with her at every turn!"

"Lies!" Lyle shouted. "And well you know it!"

"It is the truth!" Haynes stated, straightening with determination. "Why else would she have gone to such lengths? She should have killed Race as she had first meant to. He deserved no better."

"If you harbor such a hatred of him, why do you remain here?" Chalyce asked.

"To protect simpletons like yourself, Chalyce...to protect them from that brute," Haynes answered.

"Protect me?" Chalyce mocked. "You? You call attempting to force yourself on me in the smokehouse protection?" At that moment, a quiet voice in Chalyce's head revealed something to her, and she repeated it aloud. "You were in love with Melisia, weren't you?"

Haynes stood silent and unmoving. Lyle looked to him as realization dawned within his mind as well.

"Yes," Lyle agreed. "I remember. You used to pay court to her before her attentions turned to Race."

"Is that why you work for him? Pretend to call him friend?" Chalyce asked. "Are you lying in wait to kill him yourself?"

Haynes inhaled and calmly spoke, "I was to wait until the snow cleared a bit, Chalyce. But I see the time has arrived, and I must act now."

Before she could fathom what had happened, Chalyce found herself being held tight against Haynes—a knife to her throat.

"Release her, Haynes!" Lyle commanded.

"I'll not take any more orders from you, Lyle," Haynes chuckled with triumph. "I have had my fill of it! Helena has plans for our Miss LaSalle. You will tell

Race I said, 'An eye for an eye and a life for a life,' won't you?"

"Let me go, Haynes!" Chalyce screamed—but the sudden increased pressure of the knife at her throat silenced her.

"He will kill you, Haynes…or I will," Lyle threatened.

"No. Race Trevelian will die. It's time he paid for his crime," Haynes growled.

He was mad! Chalyce realized there had always been a fourth party involved in the circle tormenting Race. Haynes had been lying in wait during the passing years. And now she had presented him with the opportunity he had so long waited for: revenge.

"Release her, Haynes."

Chalyce felt hope swell within her bosom as she saw Race appear in the doorway. He still looked pale, and his shirt hung open as if he had not been able to exert the effort necessary to fasten it.

"I have a knife to her pretty little throat, Trevelian. Do not threaten me," Haynes warned.

Race walked forward until he stood directly before them. He stared at Haynes with pure and utter loathing.

"Release her, Haynes," he ordered. "If it is revenge you seek…then kill me. It will not serve you to harm her."

Haynes chuckled, however. "Oh yes, it will. To have you endure the same loss and pain that you dealt to me will be much sweeter revenge than simply killing you."

"I dealt you no such thing, Haynes. Melisia was…unstable. She tortured me much more than I ever did you."

"Alas, I cannot stay to chat, Trevelian. Helena is waiting for us," Haynes revealed.

"Helena?"

"Oh yes. You see, she tried to warn you. That beating was only a warning, Trevelian. But you are too stubborn to recognize it. Therefore, I am to deliver Chalyce to Helena…remove the temptation, as it were."

"What temptation?" Race growled.

Haynes chuckled again. "Chalyce, of course! I've told Helena everything that has gone on here these past few months. She is quite miffed, actually. Your behavior where Chalyce is concerned is too…intimate. It brings you too much hope and pleasure. We simply cannot have that."

"Leave her alone!" Race shouted, stepping forward.

Chalyce screamed, but Race barely flinched as Haynes struck at him quickly with the kitchen knife, cutting him deeply across the chest before holding the weapon to her throat once more.

"One inch closer, Trevelian…and you will watch her throat do the same," Haynes growled.

Chalyce looked in horror as the blood ran from the wound at Race's chest. Yet his attention never wavered from Haynes.

"I will kill you both if you harm her, Haynes," Race warned.

Haynes laughed as he began backing toward the kitchen door. "Do not threaten me, Trevelian. You are in no condition to champion her this time."

The snow was deep, and Chalyce's legs and feet stung with the cold induced by tramping through it. As Haynes dragged her toward Helena's residence, Chalyce fought to keep from succumbing to the frigid temperature.

"What a nice Christmas gift this will be for Helena," Haynes remarked.

"Please, Haynes," Chalyce pleaded. "Let me go. Everything is in the past, and it was not Race's fault. You know that."

"Quiet!" Haynes screeched. "One more word and I will begin carving you up before we get there!"

⁂

"Haynes!" Helena exclaimed as Haynes forced Chalyce through the front door of the villain's home. "Haynes, how barbaric! How could you treat our little guest so roughly? Why…she is frozen to the bone!"

Chalyce glared with utter loathing at Helena as she came forward, smiling sweetly.

"Come along…Chalyce, is it? Let us warm you up," Helena said.

"How could you wish harm to him?" Chalyce asked, shivering.

Helena lightly laughed. "Darling, we must do what is best for those we love, mustn't we? Race refuses to admit his passion for me. I have given him every opportunity and still…oh, he is shy, I suppose. And then you came along. We just cannot have him distracted, now can we?"

"You killed your own sister! You're mad!" Chalyce cried.

Haynes frowned, looking to Helena. "What is she talking about?" he asked.

Helena shook her head and waved the air in a casual gesture of dismissal. "I haven't the slightest notion, Haynes. She is simply babbling."

"Ask her, Haynes. Ask her why—" Chalyce began. The sharp sting of Helena's hand to her cheek silenced her for the moment, however.

"He has kissed you, has he?" Helena asked.

"Tell him, Helena. Tell Haynes why—" Again Helena struck Chalyce—the pain causing her words to be lost.

"I asked you a question, girl!" Helena shouted. "Haynes tells me that you have tried several times to seduce my Race. Is it true?"

"No," Chalyce answered, breathless with pain. "I have not."

"You have kissed him, have you not?" Helena growled.

"H-he has kissed me on several occasions, and I have returned his kisses with unfeigned fervor," Chalyce said. She restrained the tears begging for release as yet another stinging slap was administered to her face.

Helena stood seething before her—enraged—consumed with lunacy.

"It is why you told Melisia that Race did not love her, is it not, Helena?" Chalyce ventured. "You love him, and your jealousy drove you to—"

This time Helena's hand was fisted when it met the tenderness of Chalyce's face. The force of the abuse sent Chalyce plummeting to the floor, her forehead hitting a chair as she fell. The sticky moisture of her own blood trickling down her face caused Chalyce to reach toward the wound. She studied her bloodied hand as she drew it away—then met Helena's infuriated stare with defiance.

"It was more wonderful than you could ever imagine," Chalyce began, "the taste of his lips on mine when he kisses me...the warmth of his mouth...the bliss of being held in his arms while he..."

Chalyce halted her speech, horrified, as Helena seized the poker from the hearth, brandishing it above her head. Her intention was obvious: further harm to Chalyce—or death.

As Chalyce covered her head with her arms, expecting the imminent and plausibly fatal blow, she thought in despair, *I'll never see him again*. The tears she had withheld throughout the physical abuse ran freely over her cheeks.

Yet, as the moments passed, the expected pain from the blow did not come. Instead, Chalyce sensed another movement and heard Haynes's voice.

"No, Helena," Haynes said. "If you kill her now, you have lost your bait." Chalyce looked up to see Haynes staying Helena's hands with his own. "Think, Helena, only think. If you kill her now, he will not be here to see it. Remember our plan, Helena. You must keep your wits about you."

Helena nodded, her face contorting with her pent-up rage. "Take her to one of the spare rooms until we are ready!" she ordered, tossing the poker to the ground. "I cannot abide the sight of her!"

"Haynes," Chalyce pleaded as the man forced her into an upstairs room. "Listen to me, Haynes. It was Helena's fault! She told Melisia that Race did not love her! She did it with pure intention, for she knew Melisia would—"

"Be quiet, Chalyce!" he growled. "You know nothing of this!"

"Helena's in love with Race, Haynes. You know that! Please, you have to listen to me!"

Haynes did not listen, however—simply shoved her into a room, closing the door and locking it.

"Haynes! Please! Listen to me!" she cried, banging on the door with her fists.

After some time, however, she ceased her frantic pleading—for she knew it was in vain. It was only then that Chalyce turned and was horrifically aware of the room she was in.

She noticed that the windows were all boarded from the outside, thus preventing any light to enter—as well as making escape impossible. On the walls hung painting and sketches of Helena and another woman—Melisia. Chalyce went to one of the paintings and studied it. Melisia had indeed been beautiful. The sisters were so nearly alike in appearance that they could easily have passed for twins.

It appeared that Helena, in her obvious madness, had changed nothing in the room since her sister's death. Chalyce went to a small desk standing against one wall. There lay an unfinished letter—covered in dust—undisturbed. Picking up the letter, Chalyce read aloud to herself.

*My Darling Race,*

*Helena has told me the most hateful lies just this afternoon. She claims that you do not love me. She tells me that you have confessed having cherished a boundless love for her! I cannot believe this, Race…yet she is my sister and I know she would not lie to me.*

*Still, I do doubt her. I believe that she has always been jealous of our courting. Would she lie in order to destroy what we have together?*

*I know you have never confessed a love for me, but it must be so! I could not go on living if you did not return my love! I must speak to you concerning this, Race. You have never uttered the words before…but I beg you now to tell me of your love for me. I know I shall…*

Chalyce dropped the letter. Her suspicions had been founded! Helena had told her sister a lie, knowing that Melisia was unstable enough to at least contemplate suicide.

Bending and retrieving the fallen letter, Chalyce went to the door and again began pounding.

"Haynes! Haynes, please! Come at once! Please!" she cried. After several minutes, she sank to the floor, burying her face in her hands and bitterly sobbing. It was hopeless! There was no way to convince Haynes.

"It's locked! She must be in here," she heard a voice growl just outside the door.

Struggling to her feet, she called, "Help me, please!"

"Back away from the door, Chalyce!" Lyle called from beyond the locked door.

"Lyle! Lyle, hurry! They mean to kill Race!" she cried as she stepped away from the door as instructed.

She heard his body slam against the door several times before the wood around the lock finally split and the door swung open. Chalyce's hands flew to her mouth as she beheld Race standing before her, Lyle behind him. Race stood staring at her—enraged. His coat hung open, revealing his bloodied chest and the wound inflicted there by Haynes.

Striding forward, he reached out and gently ran his fingers over her bloodied forehead. "What have they done to you?" he asked in a whisper as the back of his hand caressed the welts from Helena's abuse.

"I have found the proof, Race," she whispered, offering the letter to him. "Helena told Melisia. She lied as well. Look here at what I have found in this very room."

Race took the letter from her, but his gaze lingered on her wounded face for a time before moving to read the letter.

"But they were sisters," he muttered when he looked to Chalyce once.

"They both loved you, Race," Chalyce reminded him. "And none of it was your fault."

Race's eyes narrowed. "I loved neither one of them. I only saw them as...as little else than casual friends. Even though I courted Melisia, I did nothing to encourage..." He was angry again then. "They have hurt you. Who did this to you? Haynes?" he growled.

"It does not matter. Please, just let us leave this place," Chalyce pleaded.

"You're not going anywhere, Miss Chalyce LaSalle."

Lyle and Race turned, and Chalyce looked beyond them to see the four Cochran brothers standing at the threshold of the room.

Helena appeared from behind them. "The trap has been sprung, Race darling. It is time you watched your little dove fall to the wolves."

"Helena, listen to me—" Race began.

"No, Race! There is nothing to say. You have fallen from my good graces. I gave you every opportunity to redeem yourself. Every month for the past four years I have invited you here…to give you the opportunity to confess your crime."

"My crime?" Race roared. "You wanted her dead! You knew she would kill herself. You sent your own sister to her death."

"That is a bitter, bitter lie, Race," Helena reprimanded. "How was I to know that Melisia was so simpleminded? You toyed with her…all the while knowing it was me that you wanted."

"What?" Race asked. "I never wanted you, Helena. Never. And I never will."

"Mr. Cochran, will you kindly teach Race Trevelian yet another lesson?" Helena ordered. "He must learn not to indulge in such sinful lying."

Ernest Cochran stepped forward. Chalyce felt her stomach churn at the sight of him—a tall, ugly brute of a man with dirty brown hair and ruddy complexion. To think she had almost been sacrificed to him! If it had not been for Race, what would her fate have been?

She looked to Race—the handsome, tortured man standing next to her. He had become everything to her. Her every waking and sleeping thought was of him. Her greatest desire at that moment was to be in his arms and to have him happy to be holding her there.

"Yes, ma'am," Ernest Cochran chuckled as he motioned for his brothers to follow him into the room. "You're in no condition to best us this time, pretty man. It would seem as if Chalyce LaSalle will be mine after all."

"You filthy…" Race mumbled as he lunged at the brute.

Chalyce gasped—watched as Lyle and Race fought Helena's four henchmen. The blows dealt by all the men were brutal. Although they were the recipients of many a vicious and bruising blow, Lyle and Race succeeded in rendering each Cochran unconscious or unable to defend himself further.

"Get up, you stupid mules!" Helena barked at the Cochrans, who lay groaning and helpless at her feet.

"Get out of my way, Helena. I am not averse to doing the same to you!" Race growled at the woman.

"Haynes, Race wishes to leave with Miss LaSalle," Helena said as Haynes appeared from seemingly nowhere. Swiftly, he took hold of Chalyce's arm and pulled her to him—pinning her against the doorframe and placing the barrel of a pistol against her forehead.

"Is this correct, Race? Is this how Melisia held the pistol that night?" Haynes hissed.

"That gun should be to my head, Haynes," Race said. "Let her go. You have no cause to harm Chalyce." His voice remained calm—yet Chalyce knew from the brilliant flash of his eyes that it took every shred of self-control he could muster.

"Fear not, Race," Haynes said, "for I will kill you as well. But I will shoot Chalyce first. She'll die just as Melisia died four years ago. I will spill her brains just as you did Melisia's."

"I have done nothing to you, Haynes," Race said.

"Nothing?" Helena screeched. "You are responsible for the death of the woman he loved, Race! How can you claim you have done nothing to him?"

"You're responsible, Helena!" Chalyce cried. "Listen to me, Haynes. Helena meant for Melisia to kill herself! She knew she would do it. I found this letter! Please, read it, Haynes," she begged him. "Please, Haynes…Race has the letter."

Helena snatched the letter from Race's hand as he offered it to Haynes. Crumpling the letter, she said, "It is utter nonsense, Haynes. Shoot the little tramp! I swear you're as dimwitted as Melisia. I told her Race did not love her, but she was so insipid. She always was. She intended to kill Race! 'Why kill Race?' I asked her. After all, it was her own fault."

Chalyce watched as Haynes stared at Helena. Then, before anyone could move to stop him, he turned the gun from Chalyce to Helena—firing and rendering her lifeless as she fell to the floor.

"Haynes!" Chalyce cried.

"I have misjudged you, Trevelian," Haynes said. He turned then and bolted away.

As Lyle dashed after him, the Cochran brothers only lay on the floor looking from the dead woman to each other and back in astonishment.

"Is all of this my fault, Chalyce?" Race muttered, staring at Helena's body. "What kind of devil am I that people would kill because of me?"

Chalyce took one of his bruised and bleeding hands in her own. "You are an angel, Race Trevelian…and people covet angelic beings. They want to possess them…be the recipients of their love. This…none of it is your fault."

"You have been bleeding here," he mumbled, caressing her forehead with his fingertips. "We will attend to that. But there are other things that must be attended to just now." Turning to the Cochrans, who were at last struggling to their feet, he said, "You no longer have an ally against me, Cochran." Ernest Cochran stood to face Race as he continued, "You have two paths before you. You may leave the mountain before spring…else you can be sure that the constable in town will hear of your part in this matter."

Ernest took several deep breaths, and then, clutching at his ribs, he growled, "You're cursed, Trevelian. People drop dead in your very wake. We'll be gone as soon as we are able. We don't want to be victims of the Trevelian curse!"

Chalyce watched as the vile brothers left. She then saw the doubt become visible once more on Race's face as he gathered Helena's body into his arms and gently placed her on Melisia's bed.

"I thought I would be too late," he muttered, turning to gaze at Chalyce again. "I thought she would have…that you would be dead." Reaching out, he took hold of her arm, pulling her into his strong embrace. Releasing her, he clutched her hand in his and led her from the room.

Race did not speak as he led her out of the house.

Then, as he began to remove his coat, intending it for her, Chalyce said, "No. You need it more than I. Only give me your arm about my shoulder, and we will both be better off." Lifting one of his massive arms, she snugly tucked herself beneath it.

"It is too brutal out, Chalyce. Here," he said, removing his arm from about her shoulders. He stepped behind her. The warmth of his coat as he wrapped them both in it, coupled with the elation of being near him, bathed Chalyce in euphoria!

"Match my stride," he whispered, and she shivered with delight at his breath on her hair.

"I am sorry, Chalyce," he said after they had walked a distance. "You will be haunted by your own nightmares now, no doubt." Then, sighing heavily, he added, "But perhaps I can put mine to rest at long last. I have you to thank for that…my friend."

Chalyce felt the cold penetrating clear through to her heart at that moment. The meaning in his words was as plain and cold as the snow covering the earth all around her. She had helped him to overcome his guilt, nightmares, and torment. For that he would always be thankful; for that he would call her friend. He would press forward in life now—able to go on without the constant haunting of the past devouring his soul. He would return her to her family when spring arrived, and that would be the end of his attachment to her—for, in truth, she would ever only serve as a reminder of this new tragedy of Helena and of Haynes, whom he had trusted for so long only to find the man loathed him in reality.

It was all too much! Suddenly, Chalyce understood Melisia's obsession with Race. She pitied her all the more—for she too felt that her heart might splinter into a million tiny pieces, sending slivered bits of frozen pain throughout her for the rest of her life.

She broke free of him—turned—pushed him backward, causing him to collapse into the snow.

"Chalyce? You will catch your death," he began, still sitting, looking at her, bewildered.

"Don't you see, Race?" she cried. "I am one of them!"

"One of who?" he asked, still utterly confused.

"One of those who covet you, Race. I am in love with you! Completely and irrevocably in love with you! I thought...I thought perhaps the reason you came for me...the reason you toyed with me so...was because..."

"I have never toyed with any woman, Chalyce!" he shouted.

"I do not want to be just your friend, Race!" she cried out in painful confession. "I-I want to be..."

He took hold of her hand—pulled her down into the snow next to him—wrapped her in his arms. "You do not want to be my friend? Is that it, Chalyce? Do you suppose that lovers…husbands and wives…are not friends? They must be, sweet Chalyce. Else they would know no true joy in each other's company. No true love between a man and a woman is without friendship as an ingredient."

Taking her face between his hands, he forced her to look at him and continued, "I call you 'friend' because that is what you are. I thank you for salvaging me because that is what you did. I cannot stop myself from forcing my kisses on you because my desire for you is ravenous."

Chalyce tried to turn away from him as her tears spilled over onto her cheeks—but he held her face firmly.

"Do you call me friend, Chalyce? For if you do not, I will assume that your sympathy, your kindness and understanding toward me, your concern for me, and your impassioned response to those forced kisses…I can only assume that either you merely pity me as you would a lame kitten…or that you are truly a lustful woman who only wants—"

"I love you! That is why I…" she began in defense of herself. Then realizing that she had, indeed, twice confessed fully to him, she closed her eyes so as not to meet his probing gaze.

"Blast," he muttered. She opened her eyes when he added, "I had meant to say it first." He chuckled at the perplexed expression on her face and whispered, "I feel another one threatening to gain control of my senses, Chalyce."

"What?" she asked.

"One of those forced but gladly accepted kisses you so enjoy receiving from me."

Chalyce glance away—as yet uncertain—still unable to believe she had heard him correctly.

He vanquished her doubt, however, by turning her face to his and saying, "I love you, Chalyce. I confess to you that it is the reason I nearly left you to Ernest Cochran that day in the road…though you know I never would have. I saw you, and my soul knew you would heal me. It knew you would love me and that I would be as entirely obsessed by you…as someone once was of me. Do you hear me, friend?" he whispered. "I love you."

And there—in the chilling snow—his mouth captured hers. She felt from him the unrestrained love and affection, the passion he had withheld from her on the other occasions of their kiss. And it was *their* kiss—

for they shared it one with another, and she knew their souls were melded together in it.

# EPILOGUE

"Place the flowers just there, Tommy…at the base of the stones," Chalyce instructed her young son.

"And Haynes drowned in the river, Papa?" Valerie asked.

"Yes, kitten," Race Trevelian answered as he stroked his daughter's soft auburn hair. "We found him that spring…Lyle and I. He must have fallen through the ice while eluding Lyle."

"I am sorry for them, Mama," Valerie sighed. "For Melisia, Helena, and Haynes."

"I am too, darling," Chalyce agreed. "That is why we remember them each spring…to show forgiveness…and compassion."

"I am glad Papa found you in the road, Mama," Valerie said, throwing her arms about her father's thigh.

Chalyce Trevelian looked up into the handsome face of her husband. "Oh, so am I, darling. So am I," she whispered as tears of immeasurable love filled her eyes.

"I'm glad he made you kiss him so much, Mama," Tommy added. "Lyle says Papa was always kissing you...just as he does now."

Race chuckled. "Lyle will have our heads if we are late for dinner. You and Valerie race a ways, Tom. Run along."

Chalyce stood watching their children skip through the trees—*their* children—hers and Race's. And when the baby arrived in autumn, he or she would be theirs too.

"I love you, Chalyce," Race said, taking her hand and turning her to face him.

Chalyce felt her heart leap as his familiar kiss lingered on her mouth. For years she had known his kiss, and still she melted in his arms each time he administered it—still lost her breath at his touch—still held him in her dreams at night, as well as in her arms.

When he broke from her and lovingly smiled as he gazed at her, Chalyce reached up, caressing his cheek tenderly.

"And I love you," she whispered as tears spilled over her cheeks.

Race brushed at her tears with the back of his hand. "How thankful I am that your father did not simply shoot me that day I returned you to his home."

"He saw that I loved you," she whispered.

Race smiled and drew her face to his once more.

"Kissing, is it?" Lyle chuckled as he approached, followed by the two children. "It seems as if you two have been doing nothing but kissing since I can remember!"

Chalyce giggled as the children loosed the strings of the apron Lyle had tied at his waist. As he chased them playfully back toward the house, Chalyce sighed.

"How thankful I am that it was you who delivered me from harm," she whispered to Race.

"I am the thankful one, love." Race kissed Chalyce—mingling the warmth of his mouth with her own. "Thankful that heaven delivered you into my hands," he said. "And delivered my heart into yours."

# AUTHOR'S NOTE

Just as *The General's Ambition* became known among my friends as "The Lewd Book," *Indebted Deliverance* acquired a reputation for being "The Gruesome Book"—for obvious reasons. The idea for *Indebted Deliverance* had been ricocheting around in my mind for a long, long time, but I was worried Melisia's gruesome end might wig everyone out too much. When at last I did write *Indebted Deliverance* (and finally found the courage to let others read it), I was relieved when everyone loved it! Apparently (according to my friends), the scene where Chalyce smashes Race's breakfast all over his shirt and ends up having to bathe his chest counteracted the gory part—at least for them. I do know that, just as *The General's Ambition* may be a little too unsettling to some where the General's character and intentions are concerned, the circumstances of Melisia's violent death in *Indebted Deliverance* may be a bit too disturbing for others.

Still, even for all the notorious gore, *Indebted Deliverance* is my favorite of the books included in this anthology. Maybe it's because I too like the scene where Chalyce smashes Race's breakfast on his chest. Yet I also I think it may be because *Indebted Deliverance* is rather a Beauty and the Beast type story—and you *know* how I love any Beauty and the Beast tale. I think Race may have been my first "Beast" in a way. Don't you? As I've said before, these three books were the ones I "cut my teeth on," so to speak, and I do see elements in them that were seeds for ideas and story threads I used years later.

Now, one interesting thing I'm *sure* you noticed that I really never had before is that *Indebted Deliverance* is kind of different where perspective is concerned. It begins with Race's perspective—when he finds Chalyce in the clutches of the Cochrans—and then the reader is never given his perspective again. I think the reason for this is because I wasn't yet comfortable in writing from the hero's point of view. I will say, however, this is the first book I even attempted the hero's perspective for any length of time. So I guess the firsts for me in this book were the first time I endeavored to give the reader a little glimpse of the hero's perspective, the first time I included something so gruesome as the manner of Melisia's death, and my first (although probably subconscious) Beauty and the Beast twist. Hmmm—who knew?

Now, let's address a couple of other things concerning *Indebted Deliverance*, the first (which also pertains to many of my stories, both old and new) being this. Once in a while a reader will ask me, "Why are your heroines so young? Especially in your historical books?" Well, the answer is pretty simple, so I hope you're not disappointed. Though historical accuracy lends to the ages of my heroines, the true reason has to do with my credence that every woman is eternally seventeen at heart! Oh, sure, our minds may grow weathered by experience and stress, and our bodies change when we have children and as we age. However, it is my sincerest belief that most women are still—at heart—those giddy, optimistic, giggly girls we all were at seventeen. That's why we love romance, whether in books, movies, or everyday life—because we women can still remember what it's like to have butterflies in our stomachs! We still get all grinny and enchanted when a hero kisses a heroine for the first time because, well, for one thing, women do understand that "it's all about the kissing." And for another, we enjoy those moments of wonder! We miss those moments of wonder! We know how marvelous those kisses are because our hearts are still so young. Do you know that old saying, the one that goes, "The only difference between men and boys is the size of their toys"? You know that one? Well, I say, "The only difference between women and girls is the size of their derrières"! As women, our hearts are forever young—forever thrilled by a tall, dark, and handsome waiter or pirate (or a tanned, blonde, and handsome UPS man or cowboy) who would champion our virtue and beat the wadding out of a guy who might threaten or disrespect us. While men forever dream of season tickets and speedboats, I think we women dream of goose bumps and butterflies (in the romantic sense, of course—not literally). Thus, my core reason for young heroines is simply this: age is irrelevant to us because we're all still seventeen, no matter what the mirror says. It's a universal age we can all relate to!

The second thing concerning *Indebted Deliverance* is this: Dang! A couple of the guys in this anthology get beat (or shot) to a pulp, don't they? And not just by the villains—there's a fair amount of heroines slapping heroes too! If you're wondering why, it sort of goes back to the whole "defend my honor and virtue with your life" thing we talked about before. So that goes without saying (even though I said it anyway). Furthermore, I think it may be my intrigue with, and affection for, the authors and artists of the Romantic movement, Victorian poets, gothic romance, and semi-Byronic heroes manifesting in these early stories as well. Or perhaps I had some deep-seated, subconscious regret at not having slapped some guy who once deserved it. Naw—it's the other stuff. Oddly enough, I don't know if another one of my heroines has ever slapped a hero since. Hmm? Go figure.

Usually, I wind up the Author's Note here and then add the little trivia snippets at the end. However, today I've feeling *really* wild and rebellious; therefore, snippets first!

### Indebted Deliverance Trivia Snippets

Snippet #1—The original names I had "plugged in" for the hero and heroine of *Indebted Deliverance* were actually Thomas Taggart and Faris Conston. Even though I did and do like the names Thomas and

Faris (thus, hunky Tom Evans in *The Windswept Flame* and lovely Faris Shayhan in *The Highwayman of Tanglewood*), when I had the opportunity some years ago to change the main character names before *Indebted Deliverance* was released as a novelty e-book, I took it!

Snippet #2—Race Trevelian's name has a little history of its own. Naturally, I once had a crush on a cartoon character. I know—you're thinking, *She's so goofy!* again! However, the truth is the truth, and as a small child I adored the old cartoon *Jonny Quest*! *Jonny Quest* was so different than other cartoons I watched—so adventurous—fraught with peril and tons of action! Yet perhaps the biggest draw for my four- or five-year-old self where *Jonny Quest* was concerned was a totally hot and hunky supporting character named…Race Bannon! Seriously! If you're old enough to have ever seen an original 1964–1965 *Jonny Quest* episode, then you know what I'm talking about. Right? Yep, good ol' Jonny Quest and his bodyguard and tutor, Race! What a hottie!

Snippet #3—Ahhh! The legend of the Peruvian rug! The soft white rug placed before Race's hearth—

the one that Race and Chalyce are resting on when Race reveals the tragic events of his past to Chalyce? Yep! My friend Sandy had one when we were in college (way back in 1984). We loved that rug, and one year after she and I made a "faux fireplace" out of construction paper for our dorm room wall, we placed that soft, furry rug right in front of the hearth. The whole scene was actually quite inviting—a fireplace constructed from red construction paper bricks, a roaring orange and yellow construction paper fire in the hearth. It lent a certain atmosphere to our drab little pad. We would come in from the cold after classes, prop our shoes up to dry in front of it, and sit down on that cozy little Peruvian rug and drink hot chocolate. Kevin and I even have a photograph of us kissing while stretched out in front of the fireplace on that good ol' Peruvian rug. Thus, Race's Peruvian rug is a plant—a sentimental item from the past—placed before the hearth for Sandy's sake. (P.S. This sentence from *Indebted Deliverance*— "The frigid winter air stung Chalyce's face, and she owned the sensation that her nose was constantly dripping."—is also a plant for my friend Sandy, a reference to the paranoia we both experienced in the frigid winter months while attending college in Idaho.)

Snippet #4—Kristy Jo isn't my only vocabulary-gifted friend. My friend Barbara (a.k.a. Baa Baa) could also give Merriam-Webster a run for its money. Thus, one night as the Groovy Chicks and I were hanging around at Barbara's house, she said something to the effect of, "Okay. I'll give you a word, and you have to find a way to use it in a book for me." I promptly chimed, "Sure!" I mean, how hard could it be, right? Well, knowing Barbara as I do, I should've been prepared. The word Barbara assigned was: *emasculate*. Having spent a chunk of my childhood on a dairy farm and in the company of old farmers and ranchers, I knew *one* definition of the word—further knew *that* use of it wasn't going to be an option. Thus, I actually had to think about it a minute. Still, the second definition of emasculate lends itself more to my own way of thinking: to de-masculine-ize. Basically to destroy power or vigor. So, in the end, I did find a way to use *emasculate* in a book for Barbara.

Thus, my ramblings concerning *Indebted Deliverance* are at an end—as is this anthology of my early (and pretty cliché and corny) novellas. I really do hope you enjoyed peeking into the beginnings of my writing career—or at least had a good laugh! Shortly after (or perhaps even in the midst of) writing these three rather similar, rather rough novellas, I penned my first western romance—*The Foundling*. You know it as *Desert Fire*, but that's another story for another time.

I want to thank you for enjoying moments of romantic escapism with me. Whenever I hear that someone new has enjoyed my books, I feel like I've found another friend—someone who likes to sigh, giggle, ride away on the back of a horse, and bathe in butterflies and goose bumps the way I do. So thank you. Thank you for being eternally seventeen and for knowing this one simple truth—"It's all about the kissing!"

~Marcia Lynn McClure

**To my husband, Kevin…**
*"Perfectly Imperfect"* to Perfection!
A Perfect Dream Come True!
Forever My Perfect Hero!

# About the Author

Marcia Lynn McClure's intoxicating succession of novels, novellas, and e-books—including *The Visions of Ransom Lake*, *A Crimson Frost*, *Shackles of Honor*, and *The Whispered Kiss*—has established her as one of the most favored and engaging authors of true romance. Her unprecedented forte in weaving captivating stories of western, medieval, regency, and contemporary amour void of brusque intimacy has earned her the title "The Queen of Kissing."

Marcia, who was born in Albuquerque, New Mexico, has spent her life intrigued with people, history, love, and romance. A wife, mother, grandmother, family historian, poet, and author, Marcia Lynn McClure spins her tales of splendor for the sake of offering respite through the beauty, mirth, and delight of a worthwhile and wonderful story.

# BIBLIOGRAPHY

A Bargained-For Bride

Beneath the Honeysuckle Vine

A Better Reason to Fall in Love

The Bewitching of Amoretta Ipswich

Born for Thorton's Sake

The Chimney Sweep Charm

A Cowboy for Christmas

A Crimson Frost

Daydreams

Desert Fire

Divine Deception

Dusty Britches

The Fragrance of her Name

The General's Ambition

A Good-Lookin' Man

The Haunting of Autumn Lake

The Heavenly Surrender

The Highwayman of Tanglewood

The Horseman

Indebted Deliverance

Kiss in the Dark

Kissing Cousins

The Light of the Lovers' Moon

Love Me

The Man of Her Dreams

Midnight Masquerade

The Object of His Affection

An Old-Fashioned Romance

One Classic Latin Lover, Please
The Pirate Ruse
The Prairie Prince
The Rogue Knight
Romance at the Christmas Tree Lot
Romance in Sleepy Hollow
The Romancing of Evangeline Ipswich
Romance with a Side of Green Chile
Saphyre Snow
Shackles of Honor
The Secret Bliss of Calliope Ipswich
The Stone-Cold Heart of Valentine Briscoe
Sudden Storms
Sweet Cherry Ray
Take a Walk with Me
The Tide of the Mermaid Tears
The Time of Aspen Falls
To Echo the Past
The Touch of Sage
The Trove of the Passion Room
The Unobtainable One
Untethered
The Visions of Ransom Lake
Weathered Too Young
The Whispered Kiss
With a Dreamboat in a Hammock
The Windswept Flame
The Wolf King